Simple Things

KADE BOEHME

KADE BOEHME

Simple Things
Copyright © March 2016 by Kade Boehme

Editor: Heidi Ryan, Amour the Line Editing
Cover Artist: J.K. Hogan
        http://khdgraphics.com
Published in the United States of America

This is a work of fiction. While it may include actual historical events or existing locations, the names, characters, places and incidents are either the product of the author's imagination or are used fictitiously, and any resemblance to actual persons, living or dead, business establishments, events, or locales is entirely coincidental.

Warning

This e-book contains sexually explicit scenes and adult language and may be considered offensive to some readers. For adults 18+ ONLY, as defined by the laws of the country in which you made your purchase. Please store your files wisely, where they cannot be accessed by under-aged readers.

KADE BOEHME

BLURB

Carter Darling's life has been a whirlwind since his mother was elected to the senate when he was a teen. From private school to joining the military, he tried to forge his own path while making as few ripples as possible. But an injury forced him to figure out new goals for his life. After his parents were involved a sex scandal, he decided to go back home to Tennessee to get some distance and get away from the madness.

He didn't bargain on Jeremy Beck returning at the same time.

Jeremy was finally past the rich boy angst that made for some dramatic teenage years, but he hadn't earned back much respect from his parents by playing in an indie band. Now that his band was on hiatus, Jeremy was looking for space from his unhealthy non-relationship with a band-mate, so returning home to figure out his next step seemed like the way to go.

Their initial reunion turned awkward. Carter was still holding on to hurts from their last meeting and Jeremy was trying to convince himself that Carter was still just his sister's closeted little friend. But when they open up to one another again and decide a staycation fling would be a nice distraction, they may get more than they bargained for.

For two guys who've had so much drama in their lives, it might surprise them to find that sometimes love is found in the simple things. Who knew?

KADE BOEHME

Simple Things

vii

1

"You can't really be leaving," Ella stated. "Isn't there some big PR rule about not going MIA during scandals or you give the rumors power?"

Carter Darling snorted inelegantly and continued folding his shirts, placing them in his biggest suitcase. He didn't plan on returning to New York City for quite a while.

"Besides, your parents are going to flip if you take a whole semester off."

Carter turned on his friend and roommate then. "They get absolutely zero say in how I handle *their* problem. They made the problem, they can damn well fix it. I'm not going to play smiling trophy child while they do it."

Ella huffed. "Well, you can't leave me in a lurch with the rent. That's not fair."

"My trust is going to wire payments to the landlord, same as always."

Ella pulled out her phone and started texting furiously as Carter went back to his packing. "Besides, it's my parents' names on the lease, so if you want to move out, you're more than free to do so."

She huffed behind him, again. He turned on her, again. "What the fuck's it to you, anyway? You were all team Fuck the Darlings, now you're ..." He narrowed his eyes. "Shit. Did they ask you to keep me in town?"

She glared. "It's nothing that nefarious. But Paul did call to see if I could talk you into backing down for a few days, see if you'd be there for your mother's resignation speech."

Should have known. Fucking Paul Buchanan wasn't ready to give up his gravy train with the Darlings, yet. And Carter's mother wasn't ready to throw in the towel on her political career. *The second coming of Hillary,* they called Carrie Darling, Carter's mother. Although, the Clinton scandal had been all on Bill. Both Carrie and Carter's father, Wayne, had shot their political careers in the proverbial foot this time.

"How much are they paying you?"

Ella reared back. "That's low."

"Well, you had a price tag before when I decided to come out. What'd they get you this time?"

"Maybe," Ella snapped, "I don't want my friend to self-destruct. And don't forget, you used my services as much as your parents did."

"Let's be clear. The only reason I let them do it was because my mom was getting ready for bigger things and I wasn't ready to come out publicly." Carter hated that he *had* to come out publicly. Most people got to just tell their folks and their friends and the hard part was over. But no. Not when your mother was the junior senator from Tennessee, looking to run for Governor and pass her seat on to your father.

They'd begged him to put off his official coming out for at least a year when he'd returned home for good, then pushed it back another six months after that. Only to have their own shit go public because they couldn't be as "circumspect" as they'd insisted their shamefully gay son be.

"I can't stay here. My whole life has been about them and their aspirations. I wanted to be honest, to come out. That was too much for them, though. They made me feel ashamed of myself. Now, I'm done feeling like shit, like I should hide. I want to go home and see my friends I haven't seen in almost a decade. I want to be normal for five fucking minutes. I want to be out. I don't want people thinking my best friend is my girlfriend."

"What about—"

"Enough!" She blinked in surprise at his outburst. He was known for his level headedness. "Call Paul. You seem to be tight with him. And like I said, you can always move."

"And you'll what… come out and leave me to be the girl who got left for guys?"

Carter's face heated, fury bubbling up inside him. "You always knew how this would turn out. It's also why we never blatantly said we were dating. Plus, I'm small potatoes. I'm not some rock star's kid. This'll be a blip for a week or two, then they'll focus on my parents."

"You're an idiot if you think that," she said, crossing her arms. Carter felt the sadness settle deep in his bones. His body felt as if he'd deflated, his shoulders drooping. He'd been going non-stop since everything blew up in the Darling family's collective faces less than twenty four hours ago. He hadn't had to really think about his next move. He just called up an old friend from back home and she'd offered him shelter from the storm, even if he hadn't kept in touch with her so well since he had started college three years earlier.

He didn't want to fight with Ella, but he hadn't really considered the fallout for her. He'd been so absolutely done from the moment the headlines about his parents started rolling in, he'd made a plan without much more than a text to his parents saying "so long" and "fuck this."

Ella's own posture lost its rigidity and she looked embarrassed. "Oh god, Carter. I'm sorry." He held his arms out to her and she came into his embrace willingly. "Oh, how I must have sounded."

He sighed, resting his chin on her shoulder. He wasn't much taller than her, standing only five foot nine to her five foot seven. "No, I was a dick. I didn't even think."

"No. Don't feel bad. It's been so crazy the last couple days, I got so wrapped up in the clean-up frenzy and didn't even think about how much this sucks for you."

He hummed and pulled out of the hug, returning to his packing. "I can't smile for them, not after they've been so cold and morally superior, making me feel like I was less-than because I dared to want to come out." He turned to her. "I don't want to judge them for this, but it's hard."

"I know," Ella said, still shamefaced. "It's weird, too. She's a part of the liberal party. I still don't really get how you coming out would have mattered." That was a lie, though. He'd met Ella in school, but she'd interned with his mother—who said nepotism was dead?—so she had probably gotten polls and bullet pointed memos as to why Carter should keep his mouth shut. He'd sure gotten those things.

Carter frowned. "It matters. I did kind of get it. A little." He scowled. "Fuck! See, I'm taking up for them already. I gotta… I need time away."

She studied him closely before giving a decisive nod. "Okay. But promise me you'll only take spring semester off. That's eight months to get your shit together and to let this stuff with your parents blow over. If you stay out too long…"

"I can live off my trust fund." He winked to let her know he was teasing. That was something he'd never do. He'd worked too hard to get the respect of not only his teachers, but people he'd met in the boxing world. They thought a rich kid wouldn't cut it, but he'd busted his ass over the last several years to prove that he had the chops. He didn't even want to think about how he'd be losing all that respect once his coming out was official.

One crisis at a time.

After a final trip to the closet and double checking that he had put his electronics in his messenger bag, he zipped up his suitcase and pulled on his favorite Yankees ball cap.

"Do you want me to call for the car service?" Ella asked, waving her phone. She had plopped down on the foot of his bed, looking as ragged as he felt. Her blond curls were going a thousand directions after having run her fingers through it too many times, as she was prone to do when she was nervous or frustrated. He was going to miss her, but part of him was glad to be getting away from Ella. She was his friend, once-upon-a-time his very best friend, but since she'd put her name on the dotted line of a non-disclosure agreement with Buchanan & Associates, she'd become part of The Darling Machine. Carter had put up a wall between them after that, for which he now felt guilty. It was just another reason why he really needed a break.

A very long break.

He hadn't had one at all since his time in the Army had been cut short, then he'd had rehab for his bad knee and immediately started school. It'd been a whirlwind since he had graduated high school.

"No," said Carter. "I wouldn't put it past them to have instructed the car service to drive me to D.C., and no fucking way am I sitting in the same room with them. Not today."

"Carter. They're your parents."

"And I'm an adult. Adults don't have to talk to their parents when their parents fuck up."

She grinned. "Very adult response."

"Whatever," he said, surly.

"Be careful, Ells. Call Paul *after* my flight, please? I fly out in two hours so… please wait 'til then."

"I will," Ella said on a sigh.

With that, Carter grabbed his suitcase and wheeled out, then down the elevator, and out onto 2nd Avenue, where he held his hand out to hail a cab. After depositing his suitcase in the trunk and telling the driver to head to LaGuardia, he dropped his head back against the seat and took the first deep breath he had taken since he'd woken the day before to a world gone mad.

* *   *

Carter was a nervous wreck. Now that his feet were on solid ground again, he was better, but he'd breathed a sigh of relief a bit too soon in the cab, because he absolutely hated flying. On top of the fact he'd almost been late for his flight and the turbulence had been horrible, the person in the seat next to him had side-eyed him through the whole flight because she was reading one of the many articles on his parents.

Swinging Darlings

Jesus. He hadn't read any of the articles, but he got the gist. His parents had been filmed at a swinger party. He was angry for them because they had gone to an exclusive club whose clients were all big names, expecting privacy. But he was also angry *at* them, because who didn't know that people in their position had to be even more careful than a random CEO?

They were liberals, yes, but they purported a family values, moderate image, and nothing screamed family values like "we like to fuck other couples at parties." He couldn't help being a little bitter—okay, a lot bitter—thinking back on his parents reminding him a million times to keep it in his pants and watch out for guys who might recognize him, because he wouldn't want to get outed in a seedy tabloid.

Guess they hadn't taken their own advice.

So he'd practically run off the plane and sidled up to the first bar in the terminal he could find. Sarah had texted saying she'd just gotten into Atlanta, so he had a good half hour or more to have a quick drink and gather his checked bag.

He was grateful the news wasn't playing on the screen behind the bar as he ordered his margarita from the girl at the small Chili's that was tucked in one corner of the airport. His phone immediately started popping up several voice mails from his parents, Paul, and a couple unknowns. He didn't even want to imagine who the latter might be. Wouldn't be the first time the press got his number.

He absolutely wasn't ready to deal with his folks. They could just fucking wait. He wanted to talk to them with a cooler head than he had at the moment. They would probably be furious he'd left New York, even more so that he'd officially withdrawn from the spring semester.

After finishing his margarita and letting Ella know he'd arrived safely in Atlanta, he paid his tab and made his way to baggage claim. It wasn't much longer after he'd found his suitcase on the carousel, than he heard a squeal and turned to see Sarah Beck running toward him. He let go of the handle on his bag and scooped her up when she jumped in his arms.

"I can't believe you're here!" She hugged him tight, the smell of car air freshener and coconut shampoo enveloping him. He remembered the smell well, one that reminded him of summer vacations and barbecues with hometown friends. Sarah had been his closest friend, even after his parents up and moved them across the country to D.C. and enrolled him in a private academy.

He'd spent most summers going home to stay with her family on their small ranch outside Chattanooga. Back when things had been simpler. Back before he'd come out to his parents, before the media cared about who he dated, before he'd made a small name for himself in amateur boxing.

"Hey, Sarah," he said, laughing, fully relaxing for the first time in hours.

She backed up, looking him over like a concerned mother. "Have you eaten?"

"Does tequila count?"

"No. It doesn't," she scolded. "We're going to stop for food and gas, then we'll head home. My parents are so excited you're here. They will be home in a couple of days." She grabbed the handle on his suitcase and started pulling it along. He smiled as he jogged to catch up with her. She was in business mode. He'd seen it before when Jeremy had come home from Texas a few years back. The memories took the smile right off his face. He shook himself out of that, because he didn't want to even think about Jeremy Beck right then.

Glad he was back in Texas.

Sarah kept up a steady stream of conversation as they went to the car, asking mundane questions about his life. Bless her, she stayed as far from the subject of his parents as possible. They ended up stopping at a Cracker Barrel off the interstate, gorging themselves on hashbrown casserole. Carter wouldn't lie, he'd been in hog heaven eating all those carbs.

After they got gas, Sarah was gracious enough to let him nap. He hadn't done much sleeping, but being in Sarah's company and full on fatty foods and booze, his body was content enough to let him catch a little shut eye.

Or so he'd thought. He woke to Sarah squeezing his knee. "Sorry. I hate to wake you, but I need to know where you want to go."

He rolled his head, blinking the sleep from his eyes. "What?" he asked dumbly. He looked out the window to see the familiar landscapes of his childhood hometown. "Oh, shit. I'm sorry. I didn't mean to sleep that long."

"Oh, shush. It's fine. You obviously needed it." He looked over to see her deep blue eyes looking at him with fondness and sincere worry. She'd grown up a lot since he'd last seen her. She'd also gotten a little less tomboyish. She still wore her usual jeans and boots, but her thick black hair was no longer styled in a boy cut, it'd grown past her shoulders. Her full lips had a hint of pink lip gloss, but she didn't need much makeup with her flawless complexion.

"I didn't mean to make you chauffeur."

"Old habits die hard, huh, rich boy?"

Carter snorted. His family may be old money, but Sarah's family was probably just as loaded. Her father had been a big name showbiz lawyer in Nashville before he decided he'd had enough and moved his family to Chattanooga and built a horse ranch. It wasn't a large spread, but they attracted some pretty elite clients for both riding lessons and their Paso Finos.

"Would it be a bother if I stayed with you guys a few days? Just 'til I can set up something else."

Sarah scoffed. "We'd be offended if you didn't stay. I didn't figure you'd want to be at your folks' place." Fuck no. He had no desire to stay in their McMansion. "We have a guest house and a couple of the employee cabins open. Or you're more than welcome to stay in the house. You know Daphne would love having you under foot."

Carter smiled. Sarah and Jeremy always said they had three parents: their mom, Becky, their dad, Dale, and their housekeeper, Daphne. Daphne had gone to school with Becky and Carter's mom, so the families had always been close. Daphne never had kids of her own, so she'd practically adopted Carter, Sarah, and Jeremy.

Carter felt mildly ashamed, realizing he hadn't spoken to Daphne in at least six months. "She's gonna kick my ass," he said out loud.

"Oh, she's got words for you," Sarah said with a smirk. "We do get some news here in the country," she said with a mockingly thick southern accent. "We heard about you getting hurt overseas, too. We were all kind of hoping you'd come home to recuperate."

"My parents thought rehab in New York was a better idea. And then I started school."

"Yeah, well, Daphne is gonna be most angry you're so thin from staying around all the pretty people so long."

"I am not thin. I'm all muscle. I took up boxing during my recovery. I try to keep my body fat low."

"Uh huh," Sarah drawled. "The girls are gonna be disappointed you don't fill out your Levi's like you used to."

That made Carter snort. "That's the least of my concerns."

The look Sarah shot him out the side of her eye made him shrink, but he remembered he was not playing the PR game anymore. And this was Sarah. She'd been his first kiss a million years ago, and like a sister—which was why they'd never gone further than that one kiss when they were fifteen. That kiss had been all he had needed to confirm he was as gay as he thought he was. If he couldn't like Sarah *like that*, he knew he'd never like any girl like that.

She pulled her Jeep Cherokee into the long driveway that led up to the big house. "I need to tell you something. Before we get there."

Sarah's eyes darted back to him as she worried her lip. She pulled up in a parking spot in front of the large, three story, brick house that looked as far from your typical ranch house as you could get. She turned off the Jeep and turned in her seat, giving Carter her full attention.

"Okay. Shoot."

"I hope this doesn't affect me staying here. If it does, I'll respect that. I probably should have said something earlier…"

Fuck, he hated this. He couldn't believe he'd waited until now, anyway. He didn't picture Sarah as the homophobic type, but he'd been surprised before.

"You're worrying me," she said.

"I'm, um, gay." He averted his eyes out the passenger window, watching as some of the horses ran up to the fences beside the house, eyeing the Jeep.

She punched his shoulder and he looked over, startled, and she was scowling something fierce. "You dick. You think I'd care about that?"

Carter felt his face flush. Damn his fair complexion, he knew she could see it. Her lips curled into a mischievous smile. "If you think I didn't notice you checking out Jeremy's ass every summer since you got hair under your arms—and some before that—you've lost your damn mind."

His mouth opened and closed like a goldfish.

"I just thought maybe you were all closeted. You've got that girlfriend on your arm every time I see your picture online."

"She's just a friend. It's a… thing mom and dad set up."

That made her scowl deepen. "I'm not even gonna comment on that right now." She put a hand over his where it rested in his lap. "You're safe here, Carter. I hate you stayed gone so long, but I'm glad you're here."

He smiled. "Me too."

Her eyes strayed to something behind her and she scowled again. "Dammit!"

Carter followed her gaze to see a guy and girl in rather rumpled clothes heading toward a beat up, old Ford pickup. He turned a questioning gaze on Sarah whose eyes suddenly went all big and innocent. "Oh, did I forget to mention that Jeremy is home?"

Carter's heart jumped into his throat. Yes, she'd most definitely forgotten to mention that, but she knew well enough how his and Jeremy's last parting had gone. Not bad, by any means, just... cold.

But Jeremy had been a wreck back then. Carter hadn't held it against him. Much. But he'd definitely been hurt. It'd been one of the reasons he hadn't been around in a while, he was ashamed to admit.

He cast his gaze back to the couple doing the walk of shame. "I don't get it..."

Sarah grunted. "You don't want to," she said. And immediately, Carter so got it. It made his chest ache with all those unrequited feelings and the insecurities he thought he was over. Turns out, he needed more than three years to get over it.

"Hey, don't worry about it. He's just… Jeremy." Her sardonic tone spoke volumes about her opinion on the matter.

"Yep. Jeremy," he said mildly. She smirked. Now that he was officially out to her, he figured she probably understood more than he wanted her to about his feelings on the matter. He couldn't help making his face neutral, not wanting to discuss Jeremy Beck at all. She sighed.

"Good news is, he doesn't do shit with the family." Her gaze was heavy on her brother, though, looking almost pained.

"That's… okay." He shrugged.

She let out another sigh. "Let's go get you settled in." And with that, they exited the Jeep. He cast his eyes in the direction of the apartment above the garage where he knew Jeremy's bedroom to be. He hadn't bargained on this. But in the last few years, his skin had definitely thickened, whether it be from the media, his parents being themselves, his last meeting with Jeremy, or being in the ring. He could deal with Jeremy like an adult, if he had to deal with him at all.

"Well, hello, stranger!" Carter glanced up to see Daphne coming out the front door with a wide smile on her freckled face. He wasted no time hugging her, thinking even with Jeremy around, it was nice to be home.

2

Carter hadn't slept so hard or so long in years. After a huge dinner put together by Daphne, he and Sarah and Daphne enjoyed a night of catching up. Later, he had gone up to one of the guest rooms, showered, and passed out before his head hit the pillow.

The conversation with Sarah and Daphne had been light and full of reminiscing about old times as they ate hearty southern food and drank the champagne Daphne had gotten to welcome Carter home. She remembered he always liked the bubbles. He'd forgotten what it was like to have people do thoughtful things for you just because they cared. Not that his parents were awful, they were close enough before his coming out, but gifts were usually given with some endgame in mind, or publicly to show how awesome they were.

Poor little rich boy. He rolled his eyes at the thought as he showered and shaved the next morning. He decided he wasn't ready to face the world just yet, so he left his phone on the charger while he went to take care of his morning business in the bathroom. He gave his phone a wary look before deciding he could also wait until after he'd had coffee.

Speaking of which, he could smell the fresh brew all the way up in his room, so he pulled on sweatpants and a t-shirt and made his way to the kitchen. He caught a glimpse of the time on a grandfather clock at the top of the stairs and was surprised he'd slept a full twelve hours. He hadn't done that in the longest time. In fact, he couldn't remember the last time he'd slept past six a.m., much less ten.

When he walked in the kitchen, he waved a good morning at Sarah, who was already dressed for the day. Her cheeks were slightly pink, so she'd probably been out feeding the horses already.

"Look who finally decided to get up," she said from where she sat at the kitchen island. That drew Daphne's attention from where she was doing dishes.

"Morning, sleepy head." She nudged her head toward the microwave above the range. "I left you some eggs, sausage, and toast on a plate. Just hit the button and nuke them. Coffee's fresh."

Carter grunted and both women chuckled at him before going back to their work and phone, respectively. Carter went for the coffee first, then took a seat next to Sarah at the counter.

She glanced at him sheepishly. "No paper this morning." He knew why she'd said it. It was to let him know they weren't letting him see what the hometown buzz was on their fallen heroes. He appreciated it, even if he wouldn't have looked at the paper anyway. He gave her a weak smile, then went back to his coffee.

When he went for his second cup, he finally nuked his breakfast and thanked Daphne for saving him some. "Any time," she answered. She took off her yellow rubber gloves and came over to talk while Carter ate his breakfast.

"So what're your plans while you're here? Just getting away?"

"Nope. I'm taking a semester off, maybe the summer, too."

"Woah," Sarah said, looking surprised. "Will that put you far behind?"

"Not really. I hadn't really chosen a major anyway, so mostly I'm trying to figure out what I want to do. I thought I'd be in the Army for at least another five years, so I'm playing catch-up."

"How did that work with the whole gay thing? I assume you were out."

Sarah's smile was sympathetic but Daphne turned from where she'd been working, eyes rounded. "You finally came out?"

He smiled reticently at her. He wasn't surprised she had put it together, especially if Sarah had. "I actually told my folks a while back. But they wanted me to wait instead of coming out then."

That got a deep, unhappy frown from Daphne. "Shame on them."

A warmth grew from deep inside Carter's chest. Knowing he had the support of two of the most important people in his life meant the world to him. "And yes, most of my close friends knew. Not everyone, but obviously I felt I owed it to people I was working and living closely with." He shrugged. "Not like I was hooking up anyways. Between being a senator's son and rules on fraternization, I guess it wasn't too hard for it to not be a big deal at first."

Sarah scowled, but there was a fondness in her eyes. "You and rules."

"I'm not that bad."

Daphne snorted, turning her back on them. Okay, so he really wasn't that bad, but he had appreciated structure. It had been one reason he'd hated his mom's political career more than anything: uncontrollable chaos. It was why the military had appealed to him, and it'd been one of the few times his parents had shown true approval for a decision he'd made on his own in this life. Even he would admit it was nice seeing his dad look proud of him, no matter how pissed Carter was now.

He grinned to himself as he finished eating his breakfast. Then he looked over at Sarah. "I was thinking I could help out around here. Y'all don't have to pay me, I just thought if you had anything that needed doing, I could pitch in."

"You don't have to. You know no one expects you to work for your board. You're family." That warm feeling burst through him again.

"I know. I just… want to. I want to feel normal for a while."

Sarah and Daphne shared a sad look. "And thank you. Both of you, by the way," he said. "I know I haven't exactly kept in touch, but I missed y'all."

"We know," Sarah said.

Daphne reached across and ruffled his hair. "It's okay. You've been busy. We keep up with you pretty well." She took his empty plate and put it in the sink, then turned a stern look his way. "Just don't do it again."

"Yes, ma'am," he said.

"Good to see you didn't lose your manners in the big city," a deep, familiar voice said from behind Carter. Sarah rolled her eyes, but Carter flinched at Jeremy's tone. He sounded like he was teasing, but it was almost condescending. He turned to Jeremy and almost swallowed his tongue when he caught sight of the man.

Jeremy Beck had been the boy, and then man, of young Carter's dreams. He was a wild child with a daredevil streak, yet there was something almost sweet about him—though Carter would never say that to Jeremy's face. He'd always had classic good looks, but now at twenty-five, he was a walking wet dream. His shoulders and arms had filled out, as had his chest. His tight fitting white tee showed off a trim waistline and flat stomach. Carter was surprised, though, at the amount of visible ink the man sported. Most every inch of visible skin had a tattoo. He had sleeves and knuckle tattoos. His neck was covered. He even had one swooping cursive word over his right eyebrow.

Carter tried his best not to stare, but as Jeremy walked

through the kitchen in his skin-tight black jeans, it was hard not to notice the nice swell of the man's ass and his shapely calves and thighs. He still walked with a certain swagger that was all his own, and it was fucking sexy. His jeans were rolled up a bit, showing off bare ankles above his ratty old converse that had been signed and doodled on with sharpies over every white spot available.

A dark James Dean with a rockabilly style, Jeremy was a train wreck, but he was one beautiful hot mess.

"Obviously, you forgot *your* manners," Daphne said. She pointed to her cheek, which Jeremy kissed after giving her a rakish grin. "You can't say good morning before you come taking my coffee?"

"I was surprised to see Red there." Carter blushed when Jeremy ran his eyes over him. His face probably turned the color of his hair. "When'd you get in?"

Why are you even speaking to me? Carter didn't want to start his visit out with trouble, so he took a sip of his coffee before answering. Sarah beat him to it.

"Well, we got here about the time your fuck buddies decided to leave."

Carter almost choked on his coffee and Daphne's shoulders stiffened. Jeremy's eyes flicked to Carter, who kept his face as stoic as possible, then back to his sister. "We were having a jam session."

Sarah snorted, then turned to Carter. "Me and Daphne got you a cabin set up. It's the closest to the house, but not sitting right on top of it like the guest house. Thought you might want a little breathing room."

"Oh? You're staying a while?"

Carter cocked a brow at Jeremy's unreadable expression. "For a bit."

Jeremy studied Carter for a moment before humming noncommittally and going to pour himself more coffee.

Again, Carter bit his tongue to keep from asking, "*That okay with you, Prince Jeremy?*" He didn't want Jeremy to know he was still affected by his moods, by the loss of his friendship—or whatever had happened. Carter still didn't fully understand it.

Sarah just rolled her eyes again before addressing Carter. "If you wanna get your bags, I'll take you out there so you can settle in. Then we'll talk about what work you can help out with."

Out of the side of his eye, Carter could see that even though Jeremy's back was to them, his head was cocked enough to show he was listening to their conversation. Sarah put a hand on Carter's wrist and gave a subtle shake of her head.

"Sure thing," he replied, picking up his mug. He drained the last of his coffee and went to place it in the sink. He could almost swear it had been purposeful when Jeremy's arm rubbed against his as he placed the mug in the dishwater. He glanced to find Jeremy still staring resolutely at his phone on the counter in front of him. He gave Daphne a kiss on the cheek, earning a warm smile.

"Well, guess I'll see you for lunch," he said to Daphne.

She teased her hair, which was only slightly darker red than Carter's bright red locks. Some people mistook him for Daphne's kid since they both had the red hair and blue eyes. But his skin was smooth and white, blemish free, while she was covered in freckles.

"You're definitely a member of this family, only stopping by to see me when I cook."

Carter laughed, and damn did it feel nice after the tense couple of days he'd had before he'd arrived back in Tennessee. He said his farewells, even to Jeremy, but kept his gaze from wandering back to, and drinking up more of, Jeremy.

Maybe it wouldn't be so bad. Jeremy didn't seem to be as cool as he had been toward Carter three years ago, but he didn't seem anxious to be friends again, either. And if Sarah was to be believed, Jeremy was the furthest from the kind of guy Carter had thought him to be if he was still hooking up with anything that walked.

Some things were best left in the past.

3

Jeremy ran his hands through short curls as the guy sucked him. Like a pro, the guy's mouth worked Jeremy's cock into his throat and bobbed up and down.

That didn't stop the guy's brown curls from changing to a shorter red pompadour in his mind's eye. Carter's name flitted through his mind as his balls drew up. "Fuck, I'm gonna cum."

The guy pulled off and stroked him quickly and efficiently with both of his strong, calloused hands. Jeremy's cock jerked and his head thumped back against the wall as his cum spurted out on the floor between them.

Jeremy's chest heaved as he caught his breath. "Those are some mad oral skills you got there." He had to give credit where it was due. Even if he'd been thinking about someone else. This was the first time he'd thought of someone other than fucking Troy in what seemed like forever.

Blue eyes smiled at him, and an easy grin stretched the guy's face. "You weren't so bad yourself." The sounds of the party outside filtered in through the closed bedroom door. Jeremy didn't know whose floor he'd just busted a nut on. Hell, he didn't even know the guy's name who'd just blown him. But that was what he had wanted tonight.

House parties hadn't been his scene since he was a teen. He wasn't even sure why he had come tonight. Another reason hanging out with his boys was probably not the best decision right now. But he'd had to get rid of the fucking itch under his skin, the constant feeling of being turned on. Even when he wasn't hard lately, Jeremy still felt that tingle of excited energy in his core.

Unfortunately, even that expert blowjob had only scratched the surface. Carter's face in his goddamn head still had him on edge. He could still see clearly Carter as he boxed the punching bag he'd set up in the barn, shirtless and dripping with sweat. Jeremy had wanted to lick his smooth, hairless white chest, wanted to push down those gym shorts and see the long cock that teased him through the thin fabric.

"Thanks," Jeremy said, putting his own cock back in his pants. The curly haired guy put himself away as well, and grabbed his beer off the bedside table, taking a swig. He offered it to Jeremy, who declined.

Thankfully, Curly wasn't one for awkward chit-chat either, so at the declining of the beer, he'd given another thank you and a genuine smile before heading back out to the party.

Jeremy followed behind him shortly, then ducked into the thankfully empty bathroom to pee. He hated how tense he still felt inside. It was a pleasurable tension, but equally annoying. He'd just had some of the best head he'd had in a long time, and he still was hard for Carter fucking Darling.

Jeremy stared at the spot on his arm where he had

brushed Carter's three mornings ago when he had found Carter talking with his sister and Daphne in his parents' kitchen. It'd been the last thing he had expected when he stumbled down for breakfast, seeing Carter there. He didn't know what possessed him, but he should have known better than to touch the man. He'd wondered if he still got those same tingles he had years ago whenever Carter would touch him innocently in that endearingly tactile way he had. Jeremy still couldn't process his feelings for Carter any more than he had years ago. There had been many guys since the last time he'd seen the man, but his gut still clenched, his body tingling because of that one touch. The way Carter looked at him reminded him of old feelings Jeremy thought he had put aside. And it made no god damn sense.

While Carter's expressions still sometimes gave him away—Jeremy hadn't missed the way the man ate him up with his eyes—he had lost some of his openness. Carter Darling had always been almost as precious as his last name with his soft face, marble white skin that looked as if it never saw the sun, bright red hair, and large, open blue eyes. Now, though, he seemed harder.

Definitely in the literal sense, Carter was harder. His

jaw had squared and his muscles were cut, not an ounce of excess fat on his strong, athletic frame. He looked older, stronger, and even more lickable than Jeremy remembered. A product of military training, Jeremy presumed, though he knew from Sarah's updates that Carter had been in physical therapy after a knee injury that'd ended his career in the armed services.

Jeremy couldn't think back on the day he'd heard Carter was injured and that there were no updates. It still broke him out in a cold sweat he didn't like to assess.

But Carter still had that shiny spark in his eye that was very *Carter*. When he looked at Sarah and Daphne, Carter still had that sweet boy inside that Jeremy had missed. The one Jeremy had thought for the briefest moment he might fall for. Which was stupid, because Jeremy was hard ridden and put up wet at this point, and Carter was the goody-goody who would probably follow in his parents' footsteps, all the way to Washington. With a wife, to boot.

Jeremy had always had a problem falling for straight guys. His therapist said it was probably a form of punishing himself or some psycho mumbo jumbo.

But something told him, even when he'd known Carter as a young teen, that the young Darling was not one hundred percent hetero. That didn't matter. He was entirely not Jeremy's usual type. Mostly, in that he didn't have a criminal record, didn't have a laundry list of psychological traumas, and he had his shit together. Although, as far as Jeremy knew, the guy wasn't out of the closet, if he was even gay, so the crush made some kind of sense.

Jeremy was cocky as the next guy and wasn't into the whole "I'm not good enough for him" bit. But he definitely could recognize that nothing good could come from fucking with Carter. Even if the kid wasn't sweet—too sweet, from what Jeremy remembered—and Jeremy's parents didn't think Carter hung the fucking moon, Jeremy didn't have time for complications that would come from fucking up a kid like Carter. And inevitably, Jeremy either fucked up or got fucked up when he had relationships. Which was why he didn't. His situation with his band mate, Troy, holding out for something so hopeless, was just another example of his inability to make wise decisions.

Which was why he also needed to stop flirting with Carter, because in the last two days before Jeremy had left to

come back to Nashville for a final gig with his band District &
Wild, his flirt had been strong. And Carter looked like a
cornered puppy. Who had fucking time for that shit?

Someone banging on the bathroom door brought
Jeremy out of his thoughts. Damn, he must have been more
tired than he thought, zoning out like that for so long. He
washed his hands and went back into the party. At that point,
the smell of pot was thick and beer bottles littered the floor.
He wasn't sure at what point a frat and a bunch of sorority
girls had shown up, but the party was officially no longer
anything resembling his scene.

He made his way to where his band, Troy, and Troy's
girlfriend, Macy, were holding court with a few guys they knew
from another band in Austin who'd been in town for the
small-venue music festival they'd played that night.

"Yo, Germy, where you been?" Troy asked. He
smirked when he saw Jeremy, no doubt guessing what he'd
been getting into. That the knowledge seemed to turn Troy's
crank only added to a long list of reasons he needed to get the
man out from under his fucking skin.

"I think I'm 'bout to head out, guys." He nodded at

everyone in the group, shaking the hand of the lead vocalist from the other band.

"Wanna hang out in our room tonight?" Mace asked with a flirty smile. Jeremy's stomach flipped, and not in a good way. Ever since Jeremy had found out Carter had seen Troy and Macy leaving after their last band rehearsal slash hookup, he'd felt a little pathetic and kind of dirty. And that was fucking weird because Jeremy didn't give two shits what anyone thought about his sex life. Usually.

He forced a smile. "Not tonight."

Troy's smile didn't reach his eyes when he said, "I guess the twink wore you out."

Weird. Seemed he was a little pissy. Further proof Jeremy needed to get the fuck out of there. Distance from his band and his weird situation with Troy and Macy was the whole point of spending the next couple months at home. It was time to get his head back on.

He knew it from the moment his music wasn't joyful anymore, from the moment picking up his guitar made him feel stressed rather than blissed. The hot mess that was their entire band's current dynamic had Jeremy in a weird place. He was wondering if maybe he didn't want more. And that felt strangely like growing up, which annoyed him. But time off ... If nothing else, he needed it for his sobriety.

"You know it," he said, winking at Troy and giving Macy a kiss on the cheek. "I'm heading straight home in the morning, too, so I'll catch up with you guys back in Austin in June."

He didn't know what made him say June. He had intended to go back sooner. He hadn't planned, originally, on spending five months at home with his chronically disappointed parents. But saying it felt right. They didn't have any studio time until June. One of their band mates would be visiting his mother in Guatemala until at least then, so Jeremy felt like it was a sign.

Troy and Macy both looked surprised at that, but Jeremy just tossed a wave goodbye and headed out.

* *   *

Jeremy's hands ached from the cold, but there was no helping that. January in Tennessee meant cold ass mornings, and this morning didn't disappoint. The temperature on his truck's dash display said it was just above freezing. He hadn't been kidding when he'd said he was heading home first thing. After barely sleeping because of his strange anxiety ups and downs, he'd woken before the sun was up, checked out, pointed his truck south on I-24, and drove the two hours home.

He slung equipment over his shoulder and carried it into the garage, every once in a while pausing to look out at the horses as they galloped in the pasture beside the house. Their breaths caused puffs of fog in the cold morning air, but they played and ran carefree.

"You need help?"

Jeremy turned to see his sister walking up from the main barn. She was bundled in a fleece coat and her work gloves, so she'd probably been feeding. Her cheeks were pink from the chilly air, making her pretty, makeup free face appear much younger than her twenty-one years. A swelling of affection for his little sister, his favorite person in the world, started in his chest and let itself be known in the way his face broke into a grin.

"No, I got this. Thanks, though. Go get some coffee and warm up."

She rolled her eyes and grabbed the amp he had been carrying. "Have fun in Nashville?"

He held back a derisive snort. He didn't want to explain the reaction, nor did she deserve his shitty mood. "It was okay. Glad to be taking time off for a while, though."

District & Wild had been a full time commitment, physically and emotionally, for the last three years. The band wasn't big by any means, but mainstream wasn't exactly the goal. They were a bunch of misfits who'd met at a bar in Austin, where they all lived, and decided to throw together an indie folk rock band. Most of their recording was from crowd sourcing. They'd started very small, with only a few regular gigs in bars across Austin. But after a show at SXSW, one of their songs got picked up for a national commercial for a cell phone company. It hadn't exactly catapulted them to huge notoriety, but it had gotten them enough clicks to get dozens of bar and club gigs all over the country and set them up to record their next EP.

They'd been offered a label contract for a pittance, but declined because they really liked their autonomy. They didn't aspire to be the next big thing, but it was nice being able to stop their bartending, waiting, and retail jobs, and live just this side of comfortably off the music and ticket sales.

The traveling had been nice as well. His family had money, so he'd traveled plenty growing up, but there was something magical about going from city to city on your own terms, with the music and your band, seeing a side to those cities tourists wouldn't normally see.

He'd even seen Carter once when they'd played a show in Brooklyn. It'd made Jeremy happier than it should have when he spotted that bright red hair across the bar when he'd gone off stage to get a water. Knowing Carter had seen him at his best, early on in the band and after the drugs, had made Jeremy's heart flutter.

He sighed, annoyed his thoughts had wandered back to Carter. Again. This was getting out of fucking hand. He was home, supposedly freeing himself of drama for a while— specifically the hooking-up-with-a-straight-man kind of drama.

Yet there he was.

"So, how's Carter settling in?" he asked, trying not to sound too interested.

Sarah had put away the amp and had returned to grab a suitcase from the bed of his truck. "He's good. Funny, he asked about you, too." The teasing in her eyes made him scowl, but he turned his back to her so she wouldn't see the response had gotten to him.

"I don't know why you don't just ask him yourself. I know you guys were never super tight, but I could have sworn y'all were friends once. And I'd think if I can get over him not calling for three years, you can too." She had a point.

"His girlfriend coming to visit?" *Why the fuck did you just ask that?*

"Er. Apropos of nothing?" He absolutely did not turn to see her expression, but her tone was amused. "I don't think he has a girlfriend." Her tone was dubious enough to almost make him question her, but he continued unloading boxes from the back of his truck.

"Damn, Jeremy. Planning to stay awhile?" she asked.

He turned to her finally and raised a teasing brow. "That a problem?"

"No. Not at all." She surprised him by moving in and hugging him. Jeremy was a fairly prickly person, but his sister didn't give a shit, so she forced love on him a lot. He laughed and rolled his eyes, wrapping his arms around her and squeezing her back. She pulled back and, damn her, she had that worried expression on her face. Where their parents wore a constant look of disapproval and disappointment around Jeremy—which he didn't think was all that unwarranted—he'd grown accustomed to it. Hell, he even played up to it a bit. Sarah, though, always had a furrowed brow, full of concern for him. She knew his deepest secrets, after all.

Most of them.

"Anyway, yeah. Rafe is visiting his family 'til summer and we aren't set to record for a while, so we agreed on some actual time off. I'll probably be around at least until May or June."

Her look of surprise morphed into pleasure quickly. "That's great. It'll be like old times having you and Carter around all the time."

Fuck. Carter. Yeah, like old times. Only Jeremy was sober now, and wouldn't embarrass himself in front of the kid again, hopefully. Hell, he should keep his distance, but their ranch wasn't quite big enough to steer clear of anyone that easily. Plus, being a dick and hiding out every time Carter was around would just invite questions he didn't want to answer. And, in all honesty, he didn't loathe the idea of seeing Carter. Being able to touch the man, though, was something he was still trying to convince himself he didn't want.

"Sure. We'll have slumber parties and tell ghost stories and go swimming in the pond," Jeremy teased.

She pinned him with a look that said *don't make me bring up the past.* He huffed again and grabbed his luggage. "Come on, let's get this inside. It's too cold to fuck around out here anymore."

"No shit," she agreed, cupping her hands in front of her face and blowing into them. "Oh, and fair warning, mom and dad are home. They want us all to do a big barbecue tonight to welcome Carter home." The pained grimace on her pretty face made Jeremy wish she wasn't stuck in the middle of him and their parents. She obviously noted, like Jeremy, that

37

they hadn't exactly rolled out the welcome mat when he came to ask if he could spend his time off at home. Even with the band being successful and him making his own money, they acted like he was coming home because he was broke and jobless.

He nudged her with an elbow. "Bet we can talk Daphne into cinnamon rolls."

"Oh! She can never resist the double team," Sarah said with a mischievous grin.

Jeremy smiled, thinking even if there were things about being home that had him on edge, it definitely wasn't all bad. In fact, he was pretty happy to be right where he was.

4

Carter used his teeth to undo the strap on his boxing gloves. His breathing was heavy, so he had probably overdone it a bit. His knee was sore, but not so much that he would be in a bad way, if he quit while he was still ahead. He looked up at the clock on the wall and realized he'd been at it, between the bag and his weight training, for more than two hours. He definitely had overdone it.

But his parents had called first thing, wondering how long he would be away. Then Paul had called wanting to know if he planned on making any statements about his parents, warning him off. He hadn't even been gone a full week yet and everyone was barking at his heels for him to come back and fall in line for the damage control. He'd quickly told them where they could put their open ended ticket back to D.C.

He knew people said not to come out during a fight, but he'd been approached by a friend of his at NYU who wrote for an LGBT interest blog who he was considering taking the leap with. He wasn't well known and he hadn't done anything impressive in his few years in the military, but he had put serious thought into the good he might be able to accomplish by coming out. Plus, it'd be nice to have it over and done with, no more hype and with no maneuvering for or by his parents or his mother's team.

He grabbed his water bottle and drank deeply. He needed to watch himself. Between the frustration with his parents' BS and his trying to beat his sexual tension after having only just *seen* Jeremy at breakfast that morning, he'd worked his arms into a jelly-like state.

The barn where the Becks had allowed him to hang his punching bag was the smaller of three barns. That particular barn also housed an office, a supply room, and their gym. It was no mere barn, either, but a million-dollar masterpiece. He laughed at the thought of even really considering the building a barn. Perhaps "Equestrian Home" sounded more adequate, though he doubted a horse had ever been walked through the doors. Mostly, they were all in the largest, main barn.

He gathered up his towel and shirt he'd discarded long ago and made his way into the gym area. He hadn't even realized he'd been cold until he walked into the heated room. The fluorescent lighting shone, making the white walls and laminate flooring gleam. You would think you had walked in an upscale chain gym rather than a family workout room. He was thankful for the Becks' ostentatious tastes, because he would have had to drive thirty minutes to get to the closest gym with boxing equipment.

He made his way to the showers, but found himself pausing to listen to the faint sound of music. He frowned as he sought out the source, only to stop short when he realized the sound was a radio in the room where the heated pool was housed. And there, in his perfect, naked glory, was Jeremy, floating on his back.

Carter couldn't help but stare at the long lines of Jeremy's body, his thick leg muscles, and shapely arms. His body was covered in tattoos, from his neck to his strong, big feet. And boy was he proportional. Carter couldn't stop his eyes from bulging slightly as his gaze settled on Jeremy's thick, long cock where it rested heavily on his thigh.

41

Fucking A, that thing was beautiful, and Carter wanted to kiss it to life, take it in his mouth and suck on it. Even soft, it was big.

He realized he was still staring and shook himself out of his stupor, slowly backing away from the door. But he hadn't been as quiet as he had thought. Jeremy's head popped up, and instantly he sunk in the pool and came up spluttering, but laughing with good humor.

"Sorry!" Carter called out, hoping his blush could be explained away with the cold. He was still shirtless after all, and his nipples were so hard they hurt. "I heard music."

Jeremy swam to the shallow end and stood, the water cutting off just a mere centimeter from the base of his cock, and Carter forced himself to keep his eyes on Jeremy's face. He understood why straight guys couldn't help staring at boobs if they did for them what a nice cock and a lickable Adonis belt did for Carter.

"It's all good. I tried to warn you I was in here, but you were really focused on your work out, so I didn't figure you heard me." Carter could almost swear Jeremy had raked his eyes over his bare torso, and he felt way too naked all of the sudden. God, how he wanted to dive in the pool and hump Jeremy's leg right about now. And fuck. He casually gripped his shirt with both hands in front of him, covering up the fact that his cock was getting very happy right about then.

"Uh, you always swim naked when everyone's home?" Carter didn't mean to sound as snappish as he had. But it couldn't be helped. He tried to smile like he was teasing, but the raised eyebrow and the way Jeremy's lip ticked up on one side said he might be on to Carter.

That fucking sexy tilt of Jeremy's head, the subtle way he tensed his muscles to show off, made Carter flush with desire and fucking raging need. It didn't help that he *knew* Jeremy was into guys. Whether the man was bi or gay, Carter wasn't sure, but Sarah had definitely railed about Carter's weird relationship with one of his band mates that also included a girlfriend in the mix.

"No one ever uses the gym pool except me. Sorry. I didn't think about it." He didn't sound sorry. Didn't look it, either.

"No problem. Should probably shut the door next time, though."

43

"I'll remember that," Jeremy said with an indulgent smile.

"Okay, well, I'm going to go shower for the barbecue and all…" Carter trailed off, sliding his eyes away as Jeremy slowly walked out of the pool, his thick cock flopping from side to side as he took the steps. Jeremy picked his towel up and had covered himself before Carter's eyes went back his direction. "See you there?"

"Sure thing," Jeremy responded, still smiling, seemingly to himself.

And Carter didn't wait on a further response, just turned and walked out. He made his way toward the back of the gym where the shower room was and closed himself in one of the two shower stalls after practically ripping his shorts off.

He probably should have taken a cold shower, but he didn't want to get sick. He ducked under the showerhead as the lukewarm, then hot, water came flowing down over him. As his muscles relaxed and the tension left them, his cock continued to stand straight out from his body. His mind wouldn't stop wandering to the image of Jeremy's smoothly shaven cock and hairless balls. He didn't think the bare look would do it for him, but Jeremy had tattoos all the way down to his cock's base, so it had been hot as fuck. Carter wanted to kiss and bite every inch.

Carter's cock twitched to the rhythm of his pulse as he stared down at it. His cock wasn't as long or thick as Jeremy's but it was definitely one to be proud of. The few people who had seen it, even if he had only ever had a blowjob and a couple hand jobs, hadn't been disappointed with what they had seen.

But he couldn't remember being this wound up. Ever.

He grabbed his hard on, despite himself, and closed his eyes, picturing himself laving attention on Jeremy's sexy dick. He imagined how it would feel on his tongue, how Jeremy would taste. And that did him in, stupid neglected dick. He came with a muffled shout, clenching his teeth. He stared dumbly as his cum spurted out of him and washed down the drain, wishing more than anything Jeremy was in there with him, while at the same time fussing at himself for letting his stupid childhood crush take hold again.

Who was he kidding? It had never really gone away. He remembered seeing Jeremy sing with his band at the dive bar in Brooklyn a few years ago, the way Jeremy's whole body had glowed with the passion of his music. Carter had listened to every song District & Wild had ever put out, sadly hoping even one of those songs might be for him. But he had never had the courage to do anything before, then Jeremy had shut him down, and he would never try again.

He would certainly enjoy the mental photo he had taken of the man in all his naked glory, though. At least he had that until he found someone who wanted him for more than just someone to tease to pass the time.

He needed to finally get laid. That would obviously help. He needed to say fuck it, now that he didn't have to be worried about being outed by some club fuck. Someone uncomplicated and not the brother of one of his oldest friends would definitely be best.

*   *   *

Jeremy dressed in a newer light-blue V-neck tee and black skinny jeans, even put on a little cologne. It would be the first time he really sat down with his parents since he got home, so he figured he could at least get cleaned up. Not that it would impress them any, but at least he had made the effort.

Okay, so a little of the effort was for Carter too. He wouldn't lie to himself and say he didn't enjoy the way Carter had looked at him in the pool. Carter had always had a way of looking at Jeremy that made him feel ten feet tall and that hadn't changed. Only now, even against his better judgment, Jeremy was intrigued by this cat and mouse thing Carter had started with his eye fucking and that hard cock he hadn't hidden as well as he'd thought under that t-shirt.

Jeremy always thought the guy might be on his side of the Kinsey scale, at least somewhere in the middle. But now he had some pretty irrefutable proof. Didn't mean it was wise to act on it. But it was too delicious to pass up playing with a little.

He didn't want to be a cock tease. He knew how shitty that was. He'd never actually fuck around with the guy, he didn't think, so it was probably rude as hell. But Carter clearly wanted it. Again, against his better judgment, Jeremy didn't know if Carter asked for it outright if he'd be able to turn the man down.

Not after seeing those wiry muscles up close. Jeremy was too damn tempted by all that smooth, blemish-free, alabaster skin to say no if it was ever offered.

Fuck. He was getting hard and he absolutely needed to stop that train of thought now because he had to sit through dinner with his parents and Sarah, as well as Carter, so sporting wood was not cool.

He made his way from his efficiency above their three car garage to the kitchen.

"Well, you cleaned up nice," Daphne said. He thought her smile was a bit too knowing for his comfort.

"You know mom likes us to *try* when the whole family is sitting down."

"Uh huh." Daphne didn't sound like she was buying what he was selling, so he bussed her a kiss on the cheek to distract her.

"Dad grilling?"

"Just finished up. Everyone is already in the sun room.

Head on back."

He grabbed a dinner roll from where she was plating them, getting a smack to the ass for his trouble, then ran off laughing with a mouthful of yeasty bread.

When he made it out to the sun room, his dad was already sitting at the table, which meant he was late by Beck family rules. "Sorry guys," he apologized. He didn't even flinch in the face of his dad's frown. His mom smiled her usual half-smile at him and he kissed her on the cheek before rubbing Sarah's head like she was a kid and plopped down in the chair beside her.

"It's okay," Sarah said, breaking the brief moment of tension. "Carter was just telling us about how he got into boxing."

"Oh?" Jeremy said, finding he really was interested. He couldn't help shooting a flirty smile Carter's way, which got him a slight blush and good natured eye roll that he was pleased to see. Carter had a beer in front of him, so Jeremy figured that had him a little more relaxed.

"It's no big deal, really. I'm not a contender. It's

mostly hobby."

Carter launched into a story about how he had a mentor in his early days after Basic who got him into Tae Kwon Do, which led to him seeking out more contact sports. "It does help the knee itself but it was something to focus on, something to do with myself since I couldn't exactly run anymore." Jeremy loved how Carter lit up, confident and proud as he recalled his beginnings in boxing. Jeremy thought briefly that the way Carter talked about the guy who introduced him to the sport sounded more like a crush than just a friendship. He didn't know why that mattered, but the slight pang of jealousy was undeniable.

Either way, he found himself even more attracted to this grown up Carter than he'd initially been.

"You've really come into your own, son. We're all very proud of you," Jeremy's dad said.

Jeremy bit his tongue, not wanting to ruin the moment for Carter, because Carter flushed with pleasure at the praise. Sarah met Jeremy's gaze, apologetically, because neither couldn't remember his dad having ever said that to him.

But it was true. It was obvious Carter was no longer a child. He was still young, and Jeremy figured they all had some maturing to do—Jeremy more than anyone, by his estimation—but Carter was a man now. And seeing him in that new light definitely made Jeremy's blood pump faster. Maybe he should have skipped dinner. He wasn't supposed to be mooning over Carter in front of everyone.

"Got you a hot girlfriend, too," Jeremy said, all nudge-nudge-wink-wink, trying to remind himself, more than anything, that Carter wasn't out, nor was he available to help Jeremy fuck away his stupid infatuation with Troy. Carter looked at him with a tilt of the head and everyone at the table shared a look, making Jeremy think he'd missed something. He hated feeling like he was on the fucking outside, but that was par for the course. He'd committed some faux pas, yet again, and he didn't even know what it was.

Thankfully, Daphne came in shortly after with the last of the food and they all dug in. Conversation after that was surprisingly pleasant. They discussed Carter and Sarah's schooling and Jeremy's folks' work.

Conversation again came to a halt when Carter asked

about Jeremy's band. "Do you guys have a lot of shows coming up?"

Jeremy and Sarah both looked at their parents, whose faces had gone grim. Daphne's look to them was of mild censure, and Carter looked around, realizing he'd caused the tension.

Jeremy answered him anyway. "No. Not for a while. We're taking some time off. You're stuck with me for a while." Carter turned his gaze away from Jeremy's loaded one and took a sip of his beer. Sarah's expression was blank when Jeremy looked her way. Shit. He figured she'd be around to warn him off any day now.

"Good. Maybe you'll think about doing something … grown up," his dad said.

Jeremy huffed. "Didn't you make your millions signing little nobodies like me?"

"That—"

"Guys!" Sarah snapped. "Can we not? We're celebrating Carter being here. Chill. Please."

Jeremy and his dad stared each other down, but Daphne broke the ice. "Anyone want dessert?"

Everyone accepted, except Jeremy. "I think I'm gonna go on up. I got an early start on the road this morning, so I'm probably gonna head to bed early."

Daphne sent him an understanding nod.

Jeremy said his goodnights and headed for his bed and away from family fun times. He had just opened the door to the stairs that led up to his room when Carter's voice stopped him short. "Hey, Jem, hold up."

Jeremy blinked. It had been forever since he had heard that nickname. He and Carter shared a love for British television shows and Carter, nerd that he could be, thought the British nickname for Jeremy was clever so he'd started calling him Jem. No one else ever had. And it was silly. It was especially a silly thing in the way it made his chest tighten as it did. The only other person who had a nickname for Jeremy was Troy's Germy, and somehow it always felt more of an insult than Carter's Jem, which sounded… affectionate.

He turned to Carter. "What's up?"

"Can I?" Carter pointed up the stairs. Jeremy quirked a brow but shrugged and began to trudge up the steps. When they arrived, Jeremy slid his shoes off and put them by the door, lining them up by the others.

"God, I forgot how freakishly neat you are." Carter walked in and looked around. Jeremy followed Carter's gaze. His room hadn't changed since he'd first been allowed to move up there at sixteen. And yes, Carter was right, he was very neat. Even his king size bed was perfectly made, hospital corners and all.

Carter paused and looked at Jeremy, sticking his hands in his pockets. "I'm really sorry for earlier. I didn't realize the band thing was a sore subject."

Why had Carter come up for *this*? "Carter, what are you doing?"

Carter looked surprised. "Apologizing for your dad still being a dick to you."

Jeremy's head went back in surprise, then he let out a laugh. "Old habits die hard for Dale Beck. You don't have to apologize."

"No, I do. Sarah told me they don't like that you're slumming it, or whatever."

Jeremy huffed. "Or whatever." He studied Carter for a moment. "Why are you really here, Carter?"

Carter looked at him, really looked at him. "I guess… I just…" Carter stopped, then puffed up his chest a bit, looking more like that grown up Carter Jeremy had wanted to make out with earlier. "We're both gonna be here. I wanna be friends again. I get your relationship with your parents is weird. And I get the last time we spoke was… awkward." Jeremy closed his eyes. Those last words were why he didn't get why Carter was being nice now.

"I shouldn't have been such an ass to you."

Carter shrugged. "You were embarrassed."

"You think?" Jeremy asked. Seventeen year old Carter had spent the summer talking Jeremy's ear off. Jeremy hadn't felt worthy of the hero worship. At all. And he'd been half convinced Carter was gay and half convinced Carter was dating his sister. He hadn't been sure until a year ago when his sister said, "Ew, gross," that they hadn't.

Carter had caught Jeremy snorting a few lines in the bathroom during the fourth of July party that last summer he stayed at the ranch, five years ago, and Jeremy... He had been so ashamed. He'd been tweaked out and embarrassed, and fucking devastated to see the horror on Carter's face. He'd cussed a blue streak and almost punched Carter.

So no, he did not deserve kind words.

But.

"I got clean after that." Jeremy didn't know why he told Carter that.

But then Carter's eyes got that old shine, the one that no one but Carter had ever gifted him with. "That's great Jeremy. I mean, Sarah told me you had. But I didn't realize."

"Yeah." Jeremy didn't tell how important, what a pivotal thing Carter's good opinion of him had been. He hadn't realized it himself back then, and hadn't really realized the gravity of it until this very moment. That might also be why he was so weird around Carter now, too, since Carter had once again sort of witnessed Jeremy being a dumbass—this time with Troy and Macy.

"I just wanted you to know I've followed you and your band. And, if it's worth anything, I'm proud of you." Carter's shoulders tensed. "Not that I think you need my approval or—"

Jeremy laughed, holding up a hand to stop Carter. "No. I know what you meant." And goddamn. He hadn't realized how much it would mean to hear someone he'd known so long—other than Sarah—say those words. He hadn't realized how it would affect him to hear *Carter* say those words.

"Thank you, Carter." The words were quiet enough, Carter had leaned in to hear them. They both were leaning in. The moment was almost... intimate.

"Jeremy," Carter said quietly, eyes searching Jeremy's face.

Jeremy suddenly remembered himself, though. Carter may be hot, he may be nice, but—no but. Carter was nice and sweet. Jeremy didn't do sweet. He didn't do his sister's friends. He might have a little thing for Carter. He might wanna lick the guy. But teasing was as far as this went.

But you said two hours ago if he asked.

That moment was more than asking for head in the shower, though. It was loaded with emotion. Fuck that. Besides, something was off, obviously, but he'd followed Carter too. He saw what some of the blogs who cared about Carter's parents had to say, and he was pretty sure he had noticed a girlfriend. He hadn't just been being a dick when he'd asked about her. He wondered what the hell was up with that.

Jeremy moved back, then leaned against the wall behind him, crossing his ankles and giving Carter a sideways grin. "Well. I'm headed to bed. Best run along now, straight boy."

Carter flinched back, expression shuttering. Jeremy wasn't sure if it was because he'd caught himself or because Jeremy hadn't exactly come out to Carter in so many words before, and there wasn't another way to take what he'd just said.

Carter opened his mouth to say something, no doubt to tell Jeremy to fuck himself— which he richly deserved— but Sarah's voice floated up the stairs. "Carter, your mom is calling."

Carter scowled and mumbled something like, "Two swift kicks in the nuts at once." And he was gone with heavy footsteps on the stairs and a not-quite-but-almost slam of the door.

Jeremy felt like a dick. A huge one. Part of him was still mortified over what Carter had seen years ago. Another part of him wanted to fuck Carter over his dad's desk. Then the last part of him, the self-preservation part, said that nothing with Carter could ever be just sex, if he was being honest with himself. He was giving himself whiplash over this guy, so he couldn't imagine how Carter might be feeling.

He grabbed his phone from the charging dock on the counter of his kitchenette. He typed out and sent the message before he could think on it too much.

Then he'd had enough of this day. He stripped and went the fuck to bed.

5

Carter was glad to see his embarrassing display either hadn't been as obvious as he'd thought or that Jeremy had chosen to overlook it. He was pretty sure Jeremy had been teasing with that whole flirting thing, because that seemed to be Jeremy's natural state. It'd definitely been a way to cover that the moment had obviously gotten too heavy. Though, he really wished they had cleared up that "straight boy" nonsense.

He'd meant what he said to Jeremy. He thought what Jeremy was doing was awesome. Their band was solid and Jeremy was a wonderful musician. He'd been mortified at how Jeremy's parents reacted to his question. He didn't understand them at all. He did get that Jeremy had been a pain in the ass with his rich boy angst as a teen, but wow. It still seemed extreme.

When he'd seen Jeremy's text when he got off the phone with his mother, he'd been glad he'd made the leap and tried to rekindle their friendship. *Thank you*. That was all it had said. No matter how bad Carter wanted Jeremy, he'd missed their once upon a time friendliness—even if they hadn't been the best of friends because he'd just been Jeremy's baby sister's friend.

He felt like that night had been a turning point, though. Sarah had been bitching about their dad being a dick early the next morning as she and Carter fed horses and checked salt licks—he'd been serious about earning his keep—when Jeremy came in with a tired smile, passed them each a coffee and started pitching in. Sarah had given Carter a surprised but delighted looked behind Jeremy's back that still made Carter smile.

That afternoon, Jeremy had stopped by to say a quick hello and spot Carter while he worked out in the gym before Carter went to his bag and Jeremy to his pool. And Jeremy had come again this morning, teasing a little more.

Carter didn't see Jeremy during his workout- at all that night. He tried not to be disappointed, because that'd be silly as hell. But he liked having Jeremy's attention again. Even if it was platonic.

It should stay *platonic.*

He would keep telling himself that until he believed it.

He continued taking his frustration out on the punching bag and the tread mill and whatever machine he could find. He would be back in New York eventually, and he would be officially out, so he could get rid of a lot of the bullshit tension in his veins then.

He chalked most of his wanting to sit on Jeremy's face up to the fact that he really probably needed to sit on *anybody's* face. Twenty-two years was longer than most every guy he knew had gone without more than a hand or a mouth with a fellow closet case.

Carter's shoulder muscles were a little too tense that night for the bag, so he thought he might get in the whirlpool for a while. When he got out, he had to walk through the pool room. That was where he found Jeremy, whose cock was thankfully covered by a towel, but that was about it.

Jeremy turned his head slowly toward Carter as Carter exited the whirlpool room. "Yo," Jeremy said lazily.

Then he took a drag off the pungent joint he was

holding. He smiled as he blew out a puff of smoke and scratched his flat belly as he reclined in one of the folding chairs that were set out all around the pool. He held out the joint to Carter, who shook his head, declining. He'd smoked pot once or twice, but he always giggled too much and then passed out wherever he was, and he would like to maintain a little dignity in front of Jeremy.

Jeremy must have mistaken Carter's scowl for disapproval because he started explaining, "Oh, if it bothers you, I can put it out. I don't really think grass is like…a thing, though. If you're thinking about drugs and all."

Carter laughed at the very stoned way Jeremy said that. "Uh, no. I don't have a problem with pot." He really didn't. He hadn't even thought of that. "I just am really lame when I smoke. I'll fall asleep."

"Cool." Jeremy leaned back in his chair again. "There's beer in the fridge. I don't know why. I'm the only one ever out here."

"You've said that before."

Jeremy huffed a laugh and the relaxed, peaceful

expression on his face was fucking adorable. And Carter really shouldn't stay for that beer.

"Come on," Jeremy goaded, hooking his foot under the chair close to him and pulling it nearer. "Take a load off."

Fuck it. The dude was high. Carter didn't figure he could possibly embarrass himself in front of someone who was stoned.

He went to the fridge in the corner of the room, and boy, had Jeremy been right. Aside from cases of water, the fridge held a few different kinds of beer. Tons of it. He grabbed a can of a brand he liked okay and when a whole six pack came with it, he shrugged and took them all. Sarah was gone to her school for the night, so it was just him and Jeremy. Why not kick back and enjoy? Just the two of them, just tonight.

Carter sat in the chair Jeremy had pulled over. They sort of faced each other, so Carter allowed himself to enjoy the view of Jeremy's long, bare torso with its shaved bare skin covered in several tattoos. He wanted to ask about them, but didn't know if that was a thing.

They sat silently for a moment, Jeremy toking a couple more times, Carter finishing a beer. The sounds of the water lapping in the pool from the jets and the humming of the heating unit was all that could be heard. It was a companionable, comfortable silence. Carter couldn't remember feeling quite as relaxed in such a long time.

"So what's new?" Jeremy asked after Carter had opened his second beer. He was a lightweight because he didn't drink often, so his head had a pleasant lightness.

"Well. Same old, same old." Carter waved a hand, indicating the gym.

Jeremy snorted as he licked his thumb and forefinger and used them to put his half-finished joint out, declaring that was enough. "No, I meant life. I know it's probably not something you wanna talk about, but my parents are so fucking awkward avoiding topics. I figure I may as well just say I saw the shit with your folks."

Carter sighed. "That's a shit show if there ever was one." Carter sipped on his beer again.

"That why you came to stay here?"

"Yeah, I just..." Carter sighed. "I watch my ass so close." Jeremy snorted and Carter rolled his eyes.

"Sorry, sorry. Go on."

"No. It's dumb. I just… when they told me 'keep it in your pants' and 'don't do anything you wouldn't want everyone to know,' I took that shit serious, you know?" Jeremy looked perplexed. "I was fucking paranoid. From the moment we got to D.C., it was drilled in my head how much people were watching. What happens when you mix someone with social anxiety and threats of public embarrassment? You get a hermit."

"But you did the whole Army thing, and you've boxed and shit," Jeremy pointed out.

"Dude. It's been drilled in my brain. I can't help it. And I'm a spaz. Yes, I'm more confident in general, but the paranoia doesn't just go away." Carter didn't know why his mouth was on autopilot.

As he finished his last beer, it slowly dawned on him in the way things do with someone who was buzzed that the beer was his mouth was on autopilot.

"Er. Sorry. Anyway. Why'd you take time off from the band?"

Jeremy sat up, smiling and shaking his head. "No way. You're blushing. What's this?"

"It's nothing."

Jeremy's eyes widened at the defensiveness in Carter's tone. "Do you mean you don't get play?"

Carter definitely knew he was blushing and he hated it. Fucking hated his fair complexion. He hated his anxiety. He hated how he felt about Jeremy. He picked up a third beer.

"Holy shit. Are you a virgin?"

Carter's face heated more. "No. Not... I've fooled around and all. I just haven't... No relationships." Carter put a heavy emphasis on the last word.

Jeremy snorted, but seemed to stop himself. "You're saving yourself. That's... cool."

"No, not like that. I guess it was just never convenient to do more than a quick get-me-off session." He sighed. "Call me ridiculous, but I'm not completely sold on anal anyway.

Not enough to want to trust some guy I don't know to do it the first time; add to that, it could be a horrible fuck and someone could sell it to a tabloid so everyone would think I was a bad lay on top of the slutty gay son of a family values politician." *Why are you still talking?*

Jeremy's incredulous expression was comical as he eased back in his chair. "Damn, dude. That blows. Meanwhile, your parents are rocking out with their cocks out."

Carter snorted a laugh despite himself. It wasn't funny, but it was. "Isn't it the damnedest thing? They're afraid I'll get caught, so I practically wear a chastity belt. Plus, I didn't really want my first time to become tabloid worthy. Because it's always celebrity and politicians' kids getting in the papers for crazy stuff. But it turns out, my parents are the ones who— gross, I can't even think about it. Change the subject."

Jeremy chuckled, but obliged. "I'm taking a break from the band because things got… complicated. I needed to figure out where I fit and where we go from here. The music was getting drowned out by all the other shit." He'd closed his eyes while he talked and he looked so beautiful, like a model lounging like that.

Jeremy was in a talkative, honest mood so Carter wanted to ask about Troy, wanted to ask things he had no business asking.

Carter's bleary, tipsy gaze followed one of Jeremy's big hands with its long fingers as it scratched at his chest, then landed on his thigh. Carter's eyes were suddenly glued to where Jeremy's thick cock lay, clearly chubbed under the terry cloth. He licked his lips, unable to break his stare. God, but he had been beating off thinking about that cock for days and he'd only seen it soft.

He wondered what it looked like hard.

He licked his lips again as those long fingers of Jeremy's wrapped around the clothed cock and readjusted it.

Then Jeremy's hand stilled.

Carter's eyes jerked up. Jeremy's eyes were open just slightly and pinned on him, cat like. Jeremy licked his lips before they tipped up on one side into that fucking devilish smirk. "Oh yeah?"

Carter swallowed thickly. Then he noticed as Jeremy's eyes focused downward and he followed to where his cock was tenting his own thin, wet gym shorts very obviously. Hell, the silver shorts were almost see through and he wasn't wearing a jock, so the outline of his pounding cock was blatantly obvious.

He looked back to Jeremy, whose gaze was half lidded as he sucked in his full bottom lip. "Virgin boy's feeling frisky, huh?"

Carter made an indelicate grunting noise that was part embarrassment at being busted ogling Jeremy, part hardcore arousal. That intense energy that had lived under his skin since he had laid eyes on Jeremy the first time a week ago was thrumming to the surface and his body trembled with it. Jeremy smiled so fucking dirty, all his teeth showing, and he sucked in a breath as he squeezed his cock through the towel. Carter's eyes zeroed in on the hidden cock, which was fucking big and teasing him.

Then Jeremy dropped open his towel, cock hard and heavy as it lay on his inner thigh. His heavy balls pulled up in their sac, then dropped as Jeremy's cock jumped once. Carter couldn't take his eyes off it. Fuck, fuck, fuck.

His body shook with need and excitement and his

cheeks felt hot. He knew some of this was the beer, but his own cock was so hard it hurt.

Jeremy let out a deep, quiet chuckle. "You wanna suck it." A statement. Not a question. "No photographers here."

Carter looked back up at Jeremy, who had wrapped his hand around his shaft and started lazily stroking himself. Jeremy closed his eyes, still smiling, chewing on one side of his bottom lip, head back, throat exposed.

Carter wasn't sure at which point he had ended up on his knees and right in front of Jeremy, but when Jeremy opened his eyes, they were face to face.

Jeremy gripped the back of Carter's head. "You're gonna suck it." Again, it was a statement.

Carter made the move, crashing his lips against Jeremy's. And they both sighed into the kiss. It was like their mouths had been looking for each other all along and found relief in finally touching.

Carter had kissed people before, but never like this. Their tongues licked each other, dancing in their mouths. Jeremy ran his hands through the longer hair on top of Carter's head, then grabbed it, separating them and pulling Carter's head back. His mouth attached to Carter's neck and he licked and sucked and bit his way down to Carter's collarbone, where he didn't hesitate to take a bite that made Carter hiss and his cock tense, hips thrusting against Jeremy's leg.

Jeremy put his mouth back on Carter's and freed Carter's cock, stroking it with his rough, strong hands. Carter started fucking into Jeremy's clenched fist. "Fuck, fuck," Carter hissed against Jeremy's mouth. Jeremy let out another one of those deep chuckles. Then he let go of Carter's cock and lay back on the lounge chair, taking his own cock in hand. Carter didn't need to be told, he just bent down, kissing and biting Jeremy's hip bone, then kissing the tattoo right at the base of Jeremy's cock.

His brain was officially closed for business when his nose pressed into Jeremy's silky smooth ball sac and smelled deeply the scent that was all Jeremy. He looked up to where Jeremy was staring down at him, mouth hanging open a little.

"Suck it."

Carter opened his mouth, sticking his tongue against the head. Jeremy wrapped his large hand around the back of

Jeremy's skull and cradled it. "Use your hands when you can't go down any more," Jeremy instructed.

Carter wrapped a hand around Jeremy's cock and stroked him before deciding *well, you've already gone this far*, and jumped in with both feet.

He took Jeremy's cock as far as he could. He didn't gag per se, he just couldn't go further than half the long, thick length of it. Jeremy groaned, and that drove Carter on. He had never felt as powerful as he did in that moment, giving Jeremy pleasure.

He used the spit to move his mouth and hands easily up and down Jeremy's heavy, hot shaft. He had always imagined what it might feel like to have any cock, not just Jeremy's, in his mouth. The reality was strange in that it was different than he had expected. But it was fucking hot. His own cock tingled as he rubbed off against Jeremy's shin.

"That's right. Suck me. Play with my balls, Carter." Carter looked up at Jeremy, whose eyes fucking burned into Carter, driving him on. "So fucking good."

Carter used his hands for most of the length,

concentrating his lips on the head, knowing that was where he liked to be stroked and played with. The one blow job he'd had had felt best right there. He did as Jeremy asked and played with his balls with the other hand. Jeremy's hips started flexing up.

And then Jeremy was shouting, "Come up, come up."

Carter pulled off and used his spit to stroke Jeremy from root to head, swiftly and with a twist at the head. You didn't spend this long alone and not learn a few masturbation tricks.

Jeremy's shout as his balls pulled up and his body tensed was loud, almost pained, and Carter kept stroking as white cum spurted out over his stomach and drizzled down Carter's hand. Carter stared, mesmerized as that beautiful cock jerked and came. He licked Jeremy's balls, and Jeremy let out a laugh that was all pleasure.

Then he was on Carter, pulling him into a kiss. He grabbed for Carter's cock and stroked a couple times, but before he could go any further, the tension in Carter's body let loose and he yelped into Jeremy's mouth as he came and came and came on Jeremy's stomach, on the chair, and clinging tightly to Jeremy in a gripping hold.

After a beat, they separated and started cleaning themselves off with Jeremy's towel. Jeremy stood and walked, naked as the day is long, over to get another towel. He returned just as Carter tucked himself away.

Carter felt … good. He didn't feel awkward. Though, that could be the beer talking. And as Jeremy returned with a fresh towel around his waist, he smiled lazily and lit his joint, so he obviously wasn't freaking out.

Then he pinned a look on Carter, blowing out a puff of smoke. "Carter, shut up."

"I didn't—"

"Your face is doing a hundred things. It's loud. Stop. Freak out in the morning."

Carter laughed at himself, which made Jeremy roll his eyes and smile again.

Holy shit, you just blew Jeremy Beck. You just came all over Jeremy fucking Beck.

"Shut up, Carter."

Carter laughed again and sat down to have another beer.

6

Jeremy switched off the ATV and just sat there, looking out over the old back pasture. It was one of the only plots of his parents' land that wasn't utilized. There had always been big plans, had been since he was a kid, but it sat unused and overgrown with knee-high brown grass and weeds. Out in the distance stood the old barn with its rusty tin roof, the one that had been built by the original owner of the land a good fifty years ago.

He and Sarah had always escaped back there when they were kids. Then Carter had come along and joined them as well. They would ride their ATVs back and hang out around a bonfire, or sometimes Sarah would read in the old hayloft. More than once, Carter had disappeared back there to be alone because he had nowhere else to hide when they were kids and Jeremy and Sarah had respected that that was one thing they could offer him—unconditional support and a little space.

Life had thrown so much at them all since those easier days, but that was life, Jeremy figured. Everyone had their lot.

He had woken that morning and he'd been the one who needed space. He told Carter the night before not to freak out, but here he was, the one who needed to chill the fuck out.

He hadn't done anything wrong. His phone went off, like his buddy Milo had read his mind. He read the text. *It isn't like you to overthink it. Hell, if anything, it's far healthier than that bullshit with Troy.*

Jeremy snorted. Wasn't that just the damn truth? All of it. He had never been quite so concerned over a hookup before. But it wasn't just any old fuck buddy or fuckboy from a show, this was Carter.

Milo was right about the Troy situation, too. Jeremy had been wrapped up in the weird non-threesome for way too long. Maybe that had been why he had so quickly given in to Carter. To feel good about himself while being with someone, to feel like he was actually wanted, was a nice change. Even if they had both been shocked by their actions, it had been a damn good blowjob, and Jeremy had been able to enjoy the afterglow, rather than sit back and let Macy and Troy do their thing.

He wasn't even that infatuated with Troy anymore, so much as he had been accustomed to what they had been doing for so long. In the beginning, it had been kinky and fun, then he had gotten more attached than he should have. But ever present was the fact Troy was with Macy, bisexual or not, and even if Jeremy turned him on, their sex was just a means to an end for the couple. Jeremy wasn't part of the equation.

Jeremy texted Milo back. *It's just been a while since I wanted more. I don't want to get wrapped up.*

Seconds later, he got a *Woah* in response. He was as surprised at himself as Milo. Ever since he had seen Carter again, he had felt this small part of him wanting to show Carter how he wasn't that guy who had cussed him out, who had been strung out all those years ago. Especially since he had found out Carter was gay too. There was an itch under his skin now. One he didn't know what to do with.

A buzzing sound pulled Jeremy out of his thoughts. It took only a moment to realize he was watching Carter come up on one of the ATVs. Carter didn't spot Jeremy until he had come closer, and Jeremy laughed to himself that it felt like a game of chicken, both trying to figure out who would run first.

And dammit, that really helped him lose a huge chip he'd had on his shoulder since he'd first seen Carter. What were either of them doing? They were old friends, not as close as Sarah and Carter, but still friends. They hadn't seen each other in ages, but they had gotten along well since Carter had gotten back, and now they both knew the other was gay and they obviously had something physical. Carter may have some social anxiety, but Jeremy was far from cautious. Why should they make this weird? Why should Jeremy?

If Carter wanted more, that was cool. They could make each other feel good. If Carter didn't, they could be friends again. They were going to be seeing each other regularly, so there was no sense in acting like silly angsting teenagers over the fact they'd shared a hot ass moment by the pool.

Carter must have been put at ease by Jeremy's loss of tension, because he smiled, looking a little more sure of himself—and it was sexy as hell—before continuing up to Jeremy. Jeremy's phone went off again, but he couldn't tear his eyes from Carter. He was in a hoodie that was practically painted on from the perfect V that was his trim waist to his broad shoulders. Jeremy felt his flirty smile appear on his face.

Carter pulled up beside him and cut the engine. "Sorry if you wanted alone time. I didn't know you were out here." Carter didn't have to throw the *you didn't talk to me at breakfast* out there.

"Nah, I'm good. Sorry about breakfast. Needed to clear my head."

Carter studied Jeremy, but seemed to have decided to take Jeremy at his word. "It's good. I understand." Jeremy was impressed when Carter kept a steady gaze on him as he said, "Last night was pretty intense. I get it."

Jeremy chuckled. "Yeah. Intense." He raked his eyes over Carter. "Didn't know you had that in you."

Carter looked out over the field behind Jeremy, but Jeremy didn't miss how pleased Carter looked.

Jeremy sighed. "Look, Carter…"

Carter didn't look directly at Jeremy, but out of the corner of his eye. "Uh oh."

"No. Not uh oh." Jeremy laughed and moved to stand in front of Carter's ATV, looking him directly in the eyes. It was time for Jeremy to do what Jeremy did best. Keep it simple. Keep it real. Those things had saved his ass and his sobriety. Which is why he'd told himself it was time to get away from Troy, because there was nothing simple about all that.

"Carter, I enjoyed last night."

Carter's lips ticked up. "Me too."

"I've been a bit of a jerk since you got here because I have—well, hopefully *had*—some complications in my personal life. And I didn't realize you were out, even to yourself. So I put you in the column with 'complicated shit' and tried to keep you at arms' length."

Carter nodded. "I can understand that."

"I apologize for how wishy-washy I've been. I promise it was all me." *Time to keep it real.* "When you came up to my room the other night, though," Jeremy put a hand on where Carter's rested on the handle bars of the ATV, "No one's done anything nice like that for me in a while, just to see how I was. It reminded me… You're a good guy. No bullshit, no band drama, no questions. I've missed your ass." Carter snorted and Jeremy rolled his eyes. "Not your actual ass, though it ain't half bad." He winked.

"Thanks. I think." Carter studied Jeremy in an inscrutable way, his jaw firm. It almost sucked to see Carter wasn't as trusting as he once had been. Granted, Jeremy knew he'd given Carter plenty of reasons not to trust him, but that hard look was more than just Jeremy being a flake the last couple weeks. That was a man who had been through, and seen things, Jeremy would never know; a man who'd been jaded by life, not just a couple bad run-ins with Jeremy.

"So… you're cool?" Carter asked.

Jeremy cocked his head in question.

"I won't lie and say you hadn't seemed different. I

81

want you to know I didn't hold the past against you. I'm glad you're clean and all. I just don't want to be a cause for stress. I'll stay out of your way if you need space to get your head on straight. After the stuff with your band and all."

Jeremy felt a fondness he'd only ever reserved for Carter, one he hadn't even been able to deny when they were younger. "No. You're one of the good things." He came around the side of the ATV and put a hand on Carter's face. Carter seemed surprised, but he didn't move, just leaned in fractionally. The soft look in his eyes broke the last of Jeremy's resolve and he did something he hadn't done in a very long time…

He placed a closed mouth, simple kiss on Carter's lips. It was a hello and an I've missed you, and it held no promise. But it was more than just friends. Carter pressed into the kiss after a moment of stunned stillness. Neither of them opened their mouths, it stayed a gentle meeting of lips.

Jeremy shuddered. He'd never ever been kissed like this. As much as Jeremy wasn't promising with the kiss, Carter wasn't asking. It was a kiss. And it was gentle and it made Jeremy glad he'd gotten the fuck over himself for ten damn minutes and remembered his rules.

When he pulled back, Carter had a shy, crooked smile. "Hi."

"Hey." Jeremy took a step back, taking his hand from Carter's face.

"So," Carter began. "What's this? You need space? You wanna just hang out?" That was the more grown Carter.

Young Carter was inquisitive and talkative, but rarely forward. He had the look of a man who wanted to know where he stood, and Jeremy could respect that.

"Thing is, I like simple. My motto over the last several years has been 'keep it simple and always be straight forward'. No confusion, no hurt feelings. I forgot that for a minute and got wrapped up in a not-so-healthy thing. I don't wanna be a not-so-healthy thing for you. I can't promise anything, I don't expect you to, either. But I liked being with you." Jeremy sighed and admitted out loud, "It made me feel good to be with you. I forgot it could feel good to be with someone."

Carter looked so sad for Jeremy, and Jeremy almost wished he'd kept his mouth shut. "I liked it too. Honestly. You, uh, made me feel good, too. I definitely wouldn't mind more of that. If that's what you want."

"You sure?"

Carter looked back out toward the pasture. "I know you've got a life in Austin. I have one—kinda—in New York. I'm not even sure I'm looking for something serious." Carter looked at Jeremy and his Adam's apple bobbed, obviously nervous about what he was saying next. "Cards on the table— I've been so alone for so long and I think you have too. And I trust you. I do. I hope you can trust me. And maybe, while we're here, we don't have to be so alone. Because around you, I don't feel alone, never had."

Jeremy wanted to balk. That sounded heavy. That sounded intense. But he yearned. He knew exactly what Carter meant. "A torrid winter affair we'll remember when we're old?" Jeremy teased. Yeah, he remembered Carter's love of big romantic films. Being gay himself, he hadn't wanted to stereotype Carter for them when Carter was a teen, but...

"Shut up," Carter said, flushing. There was that boy, the romantic, sweet Carter who had followed Jeremy around like he had a huge crush—the one Jeremy had let follow him because he thought it was the only way he would ever feel that warmth from the man, ever.

Part of him thought maybe they were about to get in over their heads, but why not? If they only ever got this one brief respite, this short amount of time together before they went on with their lives, why shouldn't they take it?

"I don't have to take you out for dinner before I get lucky again, right?" Jeremy asked, attempting to break their heavy stares at one another. His body was already revving up, his cock pushing against his zipper, wanting to play with Carter again.

Carter laughed and started up his ATV. "Nope. You just gotta catch me."

And he was off. Jeremy sputtered, "You fucker!" then he jumped on his ATV and was off.

When he caught up to Carter at the house, he was first off his ATV. Carter stood until Jeremy was almost to him, but took off as soon as he got close. Jeremy laughed and chased him. He knew if anyone saw them, they would remember the countless hours all three of the kids had always been chasing each other and slinging mud—literally. Though they may be surprised to see it, because Jeremy hadn't exactly been his old, playful self in a long, long time. But no one would get that this was some man-child foreplay, and Jeremy couldn't deny it was as good for his soul as it was for his libido.

Finally, he caught up with Carter where he was trying to open the door that led up the stairs inside the garage to go up to Jeremy's apartment. Too slow, Carter got pinned to the door and Jeremy showed him just how excited he was, plastering himself bodily over Carter's back and grinding his hard cock into Carter's firm ass.

He reached around to cup Carter and found him in a similar state. They both groaned and ground against one another.

"What are you, twelve again? Making me play chase?" Jeremy teased through heavy breathing.

"Thought we needed to lighten up a bit."

Jeremy smiled and suckled one of Carter's ear lobes, giving his hard cock a squeeze through their denim prison. "I like how you think, Darling."

With a flick of his wrist, Jeremy had the door open and he laughed because when the door opened inward, Carter toppled forward. Carter landed on all fours, cussing a little as he crawled and started using the stairs to help him up. Jeremy popped his ass playfully.

"Aw babe, don't get up on my account. I like you like this."

Carter scowled over his shoulder, teasing, and made

his way up the stairs. Jeremy's eyes zeroed in on the naked ass that appeared as Carter started shucking his pants on the way up. His brain short circuited. *Fuck yeah.*

He slammed the door and locked it behind him, and made his way up as he was shucking his own jeans. When he made it to the top, Carter was laid back on Jeremy's bed, naked from the waist down, stroking his long, white cock. It rose proudly from a neatly trimmed nest of bright red hair that was similar in color to the hair on Carter's head, and Jeremy smirked. He didn't think it was time to joke about carpets and drapes, though.

He dropped to his knees between Carter's open thighs, running his hands over the smooth skin there. "Fuck, your thighs are hard as rocks." He looked up and grinned at Carter's open mouth and lust filled gaze. He ran one hand up over Carter's soft, shaved balls, cupping them before stroking Carter's cock with his other. "This is too."

Carter nodded. "Please suck me."

"Oh, I definitely will. I owe you."

Carter frowned. "No, I don't—"

"Carter, hush. I want to." Hell yes, he wanted to. He eyed his prize. Carter's cock was marble white as the rest of his skin, veiny and thick. The hint of pink in the head was the only color and it looked like it was carved out of stone, one of those perfectly shaped cocks that had Jeremy's mouth watering.

He lowered his head and sucked Carter in. Both of them moaned, Carter bucking his hips up a bit. Jeremy pulled off and licked around the head, rolling it with his fist, giving Carter his most sultry look. He hadn't been this fucking turned on just watching someone get pleasure from him in a long time, if ever.

"Jeremy, please…"

Who was he to make the man beg? He took Carter back in and with a few bobs of his head, sucked him deep into his throat. Carter's back bowed as Jeremy buried his nose in Carter's pubes.

He pulled off and started stroking Carter's spit-slick cock, concentrating on the head as he licked around his balls, mumbling encouragements. Carter stopped him and pulled him up, kissing him, sliding his cold tongue into Jeremy's mouth. He loved the feeling of it, the feel of Carter clinging and their cocks now rubbing together.

Carter moaned, then grunted into Jeremy's mouth and suddenly there was hot, spurting jets of cum flying between them. Jeremy took himself in hand but Carter batted him away, using his own cum to stroke Jeremy's cock. Jeremy dropped his head to Carter's shoulder and sighed contentedly as his balls drew up and he added his own cum to the puddles between them. They rocked against each other slowly, breathing loudly.

After a moment they stilled and just lay there, kissing each other, touching. Just enjoying the moment drained Jeremy of a huge amount of tension he'd been carrying around for so long.

"Wow," Carter said.

Jeremy pushed up on his elbows and looked down at Carter's blissed out expression. "Glad to be of service." He was happy to see Carter wasn't over thinking things like he had the night before. He chose to ignore how content he was right then in a way that had only a little to do with having just gotten off.

He got up and went to grab a towel to wipe off with from his en suite bathroom. Carter stood to get dressed. Jeremy made a decision then, one he knew was probably going to keep things from being quite as simple as he intended, but it was what he wanted. "You don't have to go." Carter looked at him, questioningly. "We can watching some of those upstairs downstairs shows. You're the only other person who appreciates them like me." He hoped the invitation didn't sound as needy as he feared it might.

"You're sure?"

He was less sure after that question than he had been. But they had said it earlier. "I want to spend time with you." *While you're here* was left unsaid.

The blinding smile Carter gifted him with made him glad he'd decided to get the fuck over himself. "Sounds good."

7

Carter finished helping Sarah feed the horses for the morning and enjoyed a moment in the brisk summer cold. He could see his own breath, feel the burn of the winter air in his lungs. Unlike cold in the city, though, the air didn't feel oppressive, but crisp and clean with the sun shining down on him and the horses in the open pasture land. Even if it was doing dick to warm anything up.

Carter enjoyed helping out with the physical side of the labor that happened at the horse farm. He was able to avoid the rather upscale clients, he wasn't sitting around stewing, and he felt useful. He'd been outdoors more in the last two weeks than he had been since he got home from Walter Reed over a year ago.

He hadn't hated living in D.C. as a teen or some of the travel he had been able to do when he was in the Army. New York had even had its good points, but his soul felt like it had been recharged after some time slowing down not thinking about anything but doing his part when Sarah needed help or hanging out with Daphne while she cooked.

"I'll be damned," Sarah said behind Carter. He turned her way and followed her line of sight up toward the house where Jeremy stood, stretching, in athletic pants and a puffy vest. Jeremy smirked at them when he noticed them looking his way, flipped them off and started running down the driveway in the opposite direction, toward the road.

"I haven't seen him awake before ten a.m. since—hell, since school."

Carter chuckled and started following her toward the house. He'd already gotten in his own workout and they had been feeding for over an hour, so he was starving. He practically drooled when they opened the door to the mud room and were assaulted by the smell of breakfast cooking in the next room.

"Was that your brother? Running before noon?" Sarah's mother asked from her perch at the breakfast counter.

"That's what I was just saying," Sarah responded, making a straight beeline toward the coffee mugs Daphne held out for them. She passed one to Carter and they both sighed happily after taking sips and bussing kisses on both Daphne and her mother's cheeks.

Carter couldn't help noticing the conspiratorial look between Sarah and Daphne, though Becky was none the wiser as she glanced back down at her tablet and flicked her fingers to scroll through, telling Sarah about the day's itinerary and clients.

Carter leaned on the kitchen island and glanced out the window over the sink. It was a gorgeous day and yes, he watched Jeremy's graceful stride as he ran down the far side of the fence line and disappeared just over a hill.

His mind briefly flashed back to that powerful body being on top of his, the way the man had so much power underneath his skin but still managed to be soft to the touch. The way he used every bit of his power to please Carter.

A pleasurable shudder went down Carter's spine and he had to tear his gaze from the window and get his mind out of the damn gutter before he popped wood in the middle of the kitchen with two nosy witnesses.

Sarah was watching him, steadily. "You and Jeremy seem to be back to your old selves."

"Yeah, being home seems to be doing wonders for you boys," Daphne said with not a little hint of knowing.

He shrugged. He wasn't the best a deflecting, especially with people who know him well, but he and Jeremy had discussed this while they had laid around watching television. Jeremy had been surprisingly tactile with him, and since his mood shift the day before, he'd been much different than Carter's first day there. He was more like the old Jeremy, and Carter felt more like the old him before his parents had dragged him off to be a campaign prop for five years. He didn't know what was responsible for the change in either of them, didn't know why he felt so light—especially since a small part of him was a little bummed they were so set on just being a fling for their short stay—but he wasn't complaining.

But while lying on the bed with Jeremy's leg over his and still glowing from his first non-solo orgasm in ages, they had decided in the interest of things staying simple and drama free, they wouldn't say anything to Sarah. Not like she would want to hear about their sex lives, anyway.

"Yeah," Carter said. "We went out to the old pasture yesterday."

"Oh, wow. I haven't even been out there in ages," Sarah said, expression wistful. "Remember that time we went out there to get away from Jeremy because he was in a mood—his whole teen angst phase—and were sitting there trying to do homework and he just breezed in the barn and threw mud at you?"

"But I ducked in time because I heard him coming in and it hit you right in the face," Carter said, laughing. Daphne placed two plates filled with breakfast in front of where they were all sitting now at the counter.

"You always were a gentleman, Carter," Sarah drawled with a teasing scowl.

"Thanks, Daph," Carter said before turning his attention back to Sarah. "And hey, you grew up with him. I just assumed you could tell he was around as well as I could." Carter took a sip of his coffee, mustering a little dignity after a piece of Sarah's toast hit him in the face.

He happened to catch another one of those looks between Daphne and Sarah, and again Sarah sent him a steady gaze, one brow slightly quirked, before she dove into her breakfast.

"Well, I think it's great you're all getting along," Daphne said, and took a bite of bacon.

"We weren't ever *not* getting along," Carter said. "Just feeling each other out. I'd been gone so long and that last summer I was here, things were pretty intense."

Sarah snorted and Daphne opened her mouth to speak, but was interrupted by a, "I think what my boy, Carter, is trying to say is: Jeremy was an asshole." Jeremy had come in the front door, obviously, because he'd managed to slip in on them again.

"Recently or that summer?" Sarah asked, drolly.

"All of the above," Jeremy said cheerfully and elbowed in between Sarah and Carter, stealing toast from Carter's plate and bacon from Sarah's.

"Good way to lose a hand," Sarah said. Jeremy munched on the bacon happily, making Carter chuckle.

"Let me fix you a plate," Daphne said, going to stand, but Jeremy stilled her with a raised hand.

"No need. I'm about to head out to meet up with my friend, Milo. Got some business." Carter had a momentary flash of jealousy remembering a passing mention of Milo being a fuckbuddy at some point along the way.

He had no right to get jealous, he knew that. They'd covered a lot of rules about their little staycation fling, but no one had mentioned anything about exclusivity.

But while the ladies were distracted, Jeremy nudged Carter's shoulder with his. When Carter looked up, Jeremy winked at him, smiling boyishly, and shoved back from the counter. The simple action squashed the jealousy right there, replacing it with a frisson of warmth in his chest—and his cheeks.

"I better get while the getting's good."

"Be careful!" Daphne called out from behind Jeremy and went back to talking about a riding student Sarah apparently didn't like.

The rest of breakfast went like that; Carter laughed along at some of the horror stories of some of the more elite clients Sarah had worked with.

After finishing up and putting his dishes in the dishwasher, which earned him a pleased grin and a kiss on the cheek from Daphne, Carter was almost desperate for a shower to get the sweat from working out and the smell from feeding off him.

He'd made it out of the house with a promise to show up for lunch, and had just rounded the side of the garage on the footpath to the cabins when he was shoved bodily into the side of the building.

After an embarrassing squawk, he realized he had been tackled by a laughing Jeremy. The laughter didn't last long with his mouth descending on Carter's. The kiss was heady, desperate and sloppy. Carter was left breathless, chest heaving, when Jeremy pulled back. He stuttered out a, "Damn."

Jeremy cocked a grin. "I wanted to do that in there so badly."

Carter wanted to say he didn't necessarily mind if they confirmed what Sarah and Daphne seemed to have already figured out, but he didn't want to fuck with the moment. He didn't think this truce of theirs was that fragile, but the good mood of Jeremy's made him too happy. If being in a safe little bubble of their own made it this good, he wasn't ready to mess with that.

"Good morning," Jeremy said.

"Morning."

"When I get back from Milo's tonight, we should definitely watch more Netflix."

Carter groaned. "Oh god. You did not just invite me to Netflix and Chill."

Jeremy snorted. "Damn straight." He cocked his head. "Well… straight might be pushing it."

"You're an idiot," Carter retorted, shoving Jeremy back. "I guess so, if you won't be too tired from Milo's."

God, but he sounded like a jealous kid fishing like that. Jeremy obviously thought so as well, and rolled his eyes. "I'm taking him his amps and helping him set up his practice space, but he lives down in Georgia—Blue Ridge—so it'll be a bit of a drive."

Carter felt like an ass. "I didn't—"

Jeremy smiled happily. "Yes you did. It was kind of cute, you getting all jealous-passive-aggressive on me. Kind of."

"Sorry."

Jeremy pressed a closed mouth kiss on Carter's lips, not unlike the one they'd shared in the pasture yesterday.

Damn, if they didn't have separate lives in totally far flung states, Jeremy would be — *stop it.*

"I'm yours, for now. No need to go all soldier and drag me into your cave."

Carter blinked. "That metaphor is mixed or just plain makes no sense." Jeremy just shrugged and started walking toward his truck. Carter watched as Jeremy drove off down the driveway and tried not to swoon too much. He spent a good long time that day reminding himself of those two crucial words: for now. They'd been thrown out carelessly, but he was pretty sure they'd been Jeremy's subtle reminder that this was a right-here-right-now kind of arrangement. And hell, the arrangement was a day old, no matter how far back childhood crushes went.

Plus, Carter's life was absolutely insane these days and he was still at NYU. Hell, he didn't even know what he wanted to do with his life anymore. He wasn't in a place for a serious relationship, especially not one with someone his family was so close with, one that wouldn't just disappear and mean nothing.

He didn't want any break up to come between him and Sarah or the Becks. He'd forgotten how much they'd meant to him, how much having that second family meant to him.

For now was what it had to stay. Even if that tattooed, playful man child was the best breath of fresh air Tennessee had to offer.

Simple Things

8

"What are you still doing here?"

Jeremy turned to Milo, surprised. "I thought you wanted me to help set this shit up?" He waved his hand around the garage where they had set up Milo's equipment.

Milo shook his head, curly hair flopping from side to side. Milo was the youngest in the band, only just twenty-two recently. He was also the newest member. He and Jeremy had fucked around a while after meeting at the bar Troy and Jeremy had named the band after—The Corner Bar at Disctrict & Wild. Milo gave pretty good head, but he was a damn better drummer. They'd cooled their fuck buddy arrangement when he joined the band, not only for professional reasons, but also because Milo knew the score with Jeremy's feelings for Troy. But Milo had remained a good friend, probably better than Troy had ever been, if Jeremy was being honest.

"That was when I thought you needed a distraction. You're all pre-show, happy Jeremy now, so I'm assuming you got off the angst train and jumped your guy's bone. And I'm hoping literally."

Jeremy smirked at his friend. He felt like he'd been

doing that a lot lately, but it'd been a pretty good twenty-four hours.

Milo returned the smirk. "Amazing what getting over one's self can do."

"We came to an agreement."

Milo groaned.

"What?"

"Your 'fling' agreements."

"What?" Jeremy's brows went up. "Keeps expectations simple." Milo grumbled about his using the word *simple* too, but Jeremy pushed on. "I technically live in Texas and he lives in New York City. I'm still hung up on Troy, even if it's dumb. He's been living like a hermit. We're old friends, we're attracted to each other. We're helping each other out."

"Uh huh," Milo said with an indecipherable look.

"What?"

"You know, there're two names I've heard you say a lot over our years as friends. Especially when you talk about your sobriety. There was Carter who came first and Troy who came after. You got sober because of Carter, but stayed that way with Troy's help." Jeremy did not want to talk about this. "I'm assuming this is that Carter."

"Miles, he's just my kid sister's friend who had a harmless crush. I hurt his feelings and felt bad. Yeah, it was a wake-up call, but it wasn't love or anything." Even if he couldn't admit it, it was nice seeing that shine in Carter's eyes again. It had reappeared as soon as he had told Carter he had gotten clean and stayed that way. Carter gave him more credit than his own parents did. Hell, Jeremy thought his parents would still piss test him if they could.

"I just want you to promise me something."

"Oh, hell," Jeremy grumbled.

"Don't shut him out. I don't wanna give you advice or tell you what to do. I don't even just mean as a possible more-than-friend, but as a friend, let him … be your friend."

"Eloquent."

"Stop teasing, I'm trying to be sage and shit." Milo flipped him off and continued, "You've at least missed having him as a friend. Your whole attitude today versus yesterday says it so loud. And remember, our friendship started the same way, so sex doesn't have to end the possibility. This is your chance to be away from *all* of the drama, and if this guy's good for you, getting off or talking to… let him."

Jeremy wanted to say something glib, but of all people, Milo knew him. He'd hit it on the head. How could he say no when that was what he really wanted.

"And Jeremy, if you decide to stay home, decide D&W isn't your scene anymore, it won't be the worst thing ever. It would be worse to come back if your heart isn't in it. For whatever reason."

Jeremy had thought about all of those things. It was strange having someone say to him stuff he'd had inside, at least as far as the band was concerned. There was a small part of him that thought—whether personally or musically—he may not be able to continue to grow with D&W. He sure couldn't with Troy. He recognized him as the crutch Troy had become, and for the way he let Troy take advantage of it.

"I'll think about it," he said. Milo scoffed but didn't say anything else. He did realize one thing, though. Things had been so heavy for a while and he had felt light again; being back home, being around Sarah, being with Carter. Even the last couple weeks had been full of way more introspection than Jeremy had done in a long, long time and his mind had been silenced with Carter, he could just be Jeremy with no judgment and no expectations. They still had months before he had to get back to real life, so he thought maybe it was time to enjoy his fun with Carter and maybe think about where to go when that respite was over.

"I think I'll head out then. If you're sure."

Milo snorted. "Text me." As Jeremy picked up his keys and headed for the door, Milo started playing a Barry White song through the small speakers of his phone. Jeremy shook his head at Milo's cackling.

It'd been nice to see Milo. It was nice having Milo's perspective. Jeremy, for all his faults in the past, prided himself at taking other people's words to heart. He may not always heed their advice, but since Milo's lined up so well with his inner voice, he figured it wouldn't hurt to just… do. To feel. He hadn't let himself do much of that in a long time.

He started his truck and pulled away from Milo's little two bedroom house in the mountains of Georgia, and started for home. He even let himself smile at the thought of Carter. It couldn't hurt, right? Just for now.

***

Jeremy's mind was blissfully at ease during his drive home. Most of the trip was country roads and desolate interstate highway with little traffic and lots of trees. He even listened to local radio most of the drive; a golden oldies station with Dillon and Springsteen. He'd cracked a smile thinking of how his dad would complain about feeling old about then if he'd been along for the ride.

He fired off a text once he's gotten closer to home, letting Carter know he would be earlier than he had expected. He felt a little ridiculous for how eager he'd been while waiting for that *See you soon ;)* in reply. He was glad none of his friends were there because they would give him ten kinds of hell for the grin he couldn't keep off his face. He was definitely known for being one of the more laid-back, despite recent personal dramas among them all, but his obvious good spirits and the hard on he'd had for at least the last twenty minutes would have given him away.

What it gave away, he didn't know, but he knew it was probably more than he would want to cop to.

Jesus. You've only fooled around twice. He's going back to New York. He couldn't help it, though. It wasn't just Carter. There was a weight lifted lately, a lack of stress knowing he was going to be home with people he loved. He hadn't even realized he had needed it so bad. He hadn't really appreciated it as a kid.

After he pulled up in the drive not long after noon, he parked his truck and made his way toward the house. He thought it might be too early to grab Carter and have his wicked way, but it didn't stop him from pulling out his phone to fire off a text to him. You know, just in case.

Before he could make it to the garage, he caught movement in the kitchen window. He shaded his eyes against the sun, preparing to wave at Daphne who usually was peeping out to check on him. Bless her nosy heart. But her back was to him, though he could see her arms moving in that expressive way she had when she was talking to someone.

He got closer, not sure what exactly pulled him in, and noticed her laughing audience. Carter and Sarah were facing her, faces full of laughter. Jeremy's mother started speaking, also smiling brightly, her head switching between Daphne and Carter, her hand going out to grip Carter in that demonstrative way she had with people she loved. The whole group of them look so happy in one another's company. And though Carter sat silently smiling, his gaze was full of that wonder he always had around Jeremy's family.

The side door creaked open and Jeremy turned his attention to his dad, who walked out dressed in a suit, obviously on his way somewhere important. His dad didn't wear suits all that often since he had left contract law behind.

His dad had that adoring expression on his face as he also watched the group chattering around their kitchen island.

"It's like one of them laid an egg and they all have to cluck about it," his dad said. They didn't have many conversations that didn't turn into disagreements, but one thing they could remain good natured about were the women in their lives.

"Don't let 'em hear you say that. Sarah will go on for twenty minutes about sexist analogies."

His dad gave a chuckle. "It's good to have Carter home." He harrumphed. "Shame he's gay."

Jeremy's head snapped to the side, wide-eyed looking at his dad. Dale must have realized then how the words sounded and straightened his back, shaking his head. "You know I don't mean it like that. I don't care that he's gay." Honestly, of all things his dad had been disappointed in with Jeremy, his being gay had never registered as part of that list.

"Close as I was to his dad, we always figured it would be nice if he ended up marrying Sarah."

"Like a quaint, southern fairy tale." Jeremy noticed his dad didn't seem to hold out the same hopes for them. Of course, in his dad's estimation, Carter was probably too good for Jeremy. He may not even be wrong about it, but it made Jeremy cringe a bit inside thinking what his dad might say if he knew they'd been getting to know each other again, and much more intimately.

"Only the king and queen are usually a little less... scandalous in those stories," Jeremy said.

His dad shook his head, then spat on the ground.

Jeremy would not point out that his mother would kill the man if she knew he was chewing tobacco again.

"Yep," Dale drawled. "Those two stepped in it but good. Goes to show you never know everything about everyone." Jeremy snorted, earning a grudging side eye and grin from his father. "He looks happy here, though, doesn't he? Much better than his first few days." He looked at Jeremy. "You do too."

Jeremy wondered if that was supposed to be some kind of innuendo, and quickly started looking for a deflection. Dale put a hand on Jeremy's shoulder. "I'm glad. It's good to have my boys home." Jeremy could have been knocked over with a feather. He almost didn't believe it had happened.

His father had never been tactile, nor had he ever been very open with his feelings—other than the not-so-pleasant ones—especially where Jeremy was concerned. And almost as quickly as it had happened, it was over.

"I'm off. Gotta go into town. Go rescue the boy," Dale said, tilting his head in the direction of the kitchen. Jeremy didn't watch him go, but looked in the window again, watching the laughter, and was taken back into his memories.

Jeremy was sober for the first time in days. It sucked.

He couldn't let on how shitty he was feeling, because if his parents heard he was using again, he'd be sent back to some bullshit rehab again.

Sober moments made him wonder why the fuck he used anyway.

Coke was his drug of choice, and while it was awesome when you had it, the come down was a bitch.

"That's a good question."

Jeremy looked to the ladder that led up to the hay loft. Fucking Carter. Where'd he come from?

Jeremy had been up there so long, hidden out in the back pasture so no one could see him like this, he didn't even know what time it was or when Carter had gotten to their house. All he knew was it had to be later because the stars were out and the moon was almost mid-sky. He was shaking pretty hard too, and the temperature definitely wasn't the cause.

"What are you doing up here?" Jeremy knew he sounded snappish but he wasn't exactly in the mood for company. Especially not goody-goody closet case Carter Darling. Even if he had to admit, as the guy got older—what, was he 17 now?—he got much more handsome. Shame he was probably taking out his hidden homo issues on Jeremy's baby sister.

That wasn't fair. Not everyone was fucked up like you.

"Your sister was worried but didn't want to bother you, so I thought I'd do it instead."

"Yeah, well, you can fuck off now."

"Nah. I think I'll just look at the stars."

Annoying little fucker. *Jeremy didn't care though. He was too damned miserable to consider Carter or anything else. His teeth hurt from clenching and his stomach was tied in knots.*

"So why do you?" Carter asked after a moment of silence.

"Why do I what, Red?" Jeremy couldn't find the strength to tell Carter to fuck off when Carter sat closer to him and put his letterman's jacket over Carter's shaking shoulders. He wanted so badly to run his fingers through that red hair, to let Carter warm him up. It had been so long since he had been touched, let alone hugged sincerely. Carter still looked at him in that crazy, naive way of his that thought Jeremy was better than this, and Jeremy wanted to believe he was. In fact, he probably was.

"Yes, you are better than this. So why do you do it?" Carter asked with far too much soul for a teenager. Damn, Jeremy's mouth was running away. But he'd seen some of Jeremy's withdrawals and high times. He hadn't seen Jeremy at the bottom yet—hopefully he never would—but he'd seen enough. Not that Jeremy ran around acting like a junky, but he definitely wasn't his old self anymore.

Fuck this kid. He didn't know anything. "I don't know. Why the fuck do you still hang around our house? You have your own family." Spoken like such a mature guy. And you called him a kid. Jeremy couldn't even look Carter's way. This wasn't them, that wasn't how he treated Carter.

Carter had been around as long as he could remember. They'd been friends of a sort, even with their age difference.

"I do," Carter said quietly. Jeremy realized Carter was actually answering the question he'd asked, even though it had been a shitty one. "I have a family, but yours…" Jeremy turned to look at the side of Carter's face. Carter was sitting with his legs dangling outside the barn, sitting on the ledge of the loft, right next to Jeremy. Jeremy had thought about jumping just a moment earlier. Just because he hurt so much.

Carter turned those big blue eyes Jeremy's way and he was smiling shyly. "Yours is loud and you all laugh and you all love so hard."

Carter looked back out at the stars. "I come here and I feel like you guys care. Well, your family, anyway." That stung in a way Jeremy hadn't thought it would.

"Last Christmas, you know where I was?"

Jeremy didn't know, didn't know why Carter was even asking. Honestly, he felt too shitty to answer. Until Carter answered his own question. "Alone. I was sitting at home alone. My mom had appearances and my dad had an agenda. So I left boarding school to go home for the holiday so I wouldn't be alone. But still… I was alone. And all I could think was that I wished I'd come here because it's loud and fun and I would have a laugh with your sister and your dad would sneak out to spit tobacco, like we don't know he's doing it, and your parents would fight over it. And it would feel like family."

After Carter finished, they sat quietly for a long moment. Jeremy, if he was even capable of it, felt this blossom of deep affection for the guy. Fucking Carter Darling. Precious like his name. Jeremy stared at Carter for a moment and let himself think about if things were different…

"So. Why do you do it?"

"What?" Jeremy asked, lost.

"I told you my sob story. What's yours?"

Jeremy laughed shakily at that, and how could he not answer now? "I'm an asshole."

Carter laughed, then put his hand over his mouth like he hadn't meant to. "Well, we know that much."

"No. I mean, that's why I started. I just started while I was hanging out with friends. And I won't lie, we're all just a bunch of bored

rich kids with rich kids' problems. And I tried to quit. But it sucks so bad." As if to prove the point, his body wracked with a violent shudder, but he stilled a bit after that. He had never been this candid about why he started using drugs. He wasn't sure he had even realized it until now. And he would admit, it was exactly as stupid as it sounded, especially for how shitty he felt.

"Mostly, it's because my family is loud and because they smile and I feel like an outsider. I feel so detached and I want to hurt them."

Carter put a hand on Jeremy's shoulder, and Jeremy realized he was crying. He looked at Carter, feeling like the biggest fucking idiot. And how did this kid do that to him? How'd he pull that shit out just because?

"Jeremy?"

"Yeah?" Jeremy sniffled, knowing he sounded pitiful.

"That's dumb."

Jeremy couldn't help it. He honest to goodness guffawed. Loud.

Carter handed him a king size chocolate bar. "Daphne sent this for you." Carter stood and started brushing off his pants.

"I hope you can laugh with them one day," Carter said. Jeremy blinked owlishly, surprised by the poignancy of the words, and watched Carter slip down the ladder, then followed his progress as he walked down the path toward the house.

Jeremy was pulled from his memories by a movement. He realized Daphne had turned his way and, with a wide smile on her face, she waved him inside. He saw Carter cast a wink his way.

He knew Carter had heard his music, but he wondered if Carter noticed that song, one of the few he had written himself. It had been inspired by what Carter had said, it was a song about a boy who looked inside the windows, wishing he could smile too.

Jeremy hadn't even thought about that song in ages. And he didn't know why he was suddenly so sentimental. But he did think he was ready to go inside where the people were smiling.

He walked in the door. "Hello, family unit. Are we discussing what an asshole I am again?" he asked. His mother cried foul over his language and Sarah rolled her eyes. But Carter smiled his exasperated, sweet smile that was just for him, complete with a flutter of strawberry blond lashes that had Jeremy's sentimental side flying out the window and his other head engaging its upright position.

He moved right beside Carter, joining in the conversation with them. He made sure to rub his forearm against Carter's more than once. If they were going to have to wait until later, he wasn't going to be the only one hiding a boner.

9

"I swear to god, you've been torturing me all afternoon," Carter said into the kiss as Jeremy pinned him to the wall in Jeremy's bedroom.

"Anticipation and all that," Jeremy growled breathily.

"Asshole," Carter retorted, then licked into Jeremy's mouth. They were peeling clothes off one another. No time to tease anymore. They'd spent almost the entire afternoon with Jeremy's mother, Daphne, and Sarah. Carter was happy to see Jeremy and his mother getting along so well. She'd looked surprised and pleased when Jeremy agreed to join in their game of cards with only token grumbling about how lame playing cards was.

But they'd been bumping into one another for hours. Jeremy purposefully groped Carter a few times when no one was looking. It'd been bad enough while Jeremy had been gone all morning, Carter thought about Jeremy's offer to fool around that night. But having Jeremy tease him for hours when he could do nothing about it had been fucking torture.

"You're a bastard," Carter said with feeling.

"I intend to make it up to you." Their mouths came

back together, their kisses sloppy and graceless. Their bare chests together were slick with a fine sheen of sweat, despite the chilliness of the room.

"Good," Carter sighed into the kiss as Jeremy shoved Carter's underwear down and grabbed their cocks in his fist, stroking them together, flicking the underside of their cockheads together where the frenulum met circumcised flesh. It made Carter's whole body sing.

"Damn, you're so sexy," Jeremy said, and dropped his mouth to the base of Carter's neck, sucking gently. He wrapped his arms around Jeremy's waist and gripped his muscled ass tightly.

Their hips snapped as they fucked into Jeremy's fist. "Me?" Carter scoffed. "You're fucking amazing." He couldn't even be embarrassed about being so forward. His dick was in the man's hand and the words made Jeremy's heated gaze burn brighter.

Carter sucked in Jeremy's bottom lip and suckled it. His balls were already pulling up. "Oh, shit, Jem. You gotta slow down. I'm gonna…"

"Do it. We've got all fucking night." Jeremy put his lips right up to Carter's and stared in Carter's eyes, his own eyes smiling. "You know you wanna shoot all over me. I want your cum, Carter. Get messy." Carter opened his mouth to shout his release, but Jeremy swallowed the shout, covering Carter's mouth with his own. Carter's cock jerked, spurting cum over Jeremy's fist, over Jeremy's cock, making squishy noises as Jeremy continued stroking. Carter clung to Jeremy's shoulders with both hands, riding his knee-buckling orgasm all the way out.

He dipped one hand down to cup Jeremy's balls, taking over the kiss and moaning loudly. That did Jeremy in. His cock jerked next to Carter's, making Carter moan even more, loving the feel of it. Then Jeremy's hot cum was dribbling over Carter's cock, down his balls, and that started tickling at the same time Jeremy's strong hand was just a bit much on his sensitive skin, and he fought between the urge to laugh and shove Jeremy off him. He hissed and grabbed Jeremy's clenching fist, stilling him.

"Sorry," Jeremy said on a breath, leaning into Carter, his chin on Carter's shoulder. Carter soaked in the moment. If someone walked in, they would probably think they looked ridiculous with their pants around their ankles, underwear at their knees, with Jeremy supporting himself on Carter. But Carter felt warm and content and spent for now. It was nice not jumping and running. And that it was Jeremy, who was about his same size, whose body fit just right with his.

"No problem," Carter said dumbly. Jeremy grunt-laughed as he pushed himself off Carter. He reached for a towel that was folded on the armchair beside them.

"Better prepared this time," Jeremy declared, wiping his own stomach and cock off before handing the towel to Carter. Carter got little flutters in his stomach at the thought of Jeremy being "prepared" for a next time.

But you're fuck buddies, of course he would be prepared for your visit.

Carter bent to pull his pants up, but Jeremy shoved a

pair of sweatpants at him with a playful grin. "Don't even bother. I locked the doors. Sarah's gone to see that guy she's been texting. You're gonna hang out right here, and I don't want to have a hard time if I was to hold your junk while we watch TV.

"Can't you just hold your own?" Carter was mostly teasing. He definitely wouldn't object to Jeremy holding his junk again.

"Holding yours is more fun." He pinched Carter's nipple and twisted, and was gone before Carter could react.

"Asshole," Carter grumbled.

"So you've said," Jeremy called from the bathroom. He came out holding a joint. "I'm gonna step out and hit this a couple times. There's probably beer in the garage refrigerator if you want."

Carter shrugged and nodded toward the dorm fridge Jeremy had in the corner beside his chest of drawers. "You still have soda in there?"

Jeremy smiled and confirmed he'd even brought up Carter's "gross diet soda", just in case. Again, Carter felt a little flutter in his belly when he made his way over to get a drink.

Carter couldn't believe the difference in Jeremy. He wasn't going to look a gift horse in the mouth, but it seemed even his trip to see his friend had gotten the excess tension out of his system.

It was like *Jeremy* was back. The real, sweet, playful Jeremy who'd gotten buried under a pile of coke so long ago.

Carter looked over some of the framed things Jeremy had on his shelves. He was surprised, since Jeremy had his own home in Austin, to find that he had so many recent photos up. There was even a framed printed out screen shot of when District & Wild's one song had gone to number 1 on an iTunes chart.

He smiled to himself when he noticed a photo of Jeremy, Sarah, and himself at a horse show when Carter was sixteen. He was a little surprised at how warmly then eighteen year old Jeremy was looking at him. It almost looked like a crush, but he dared not think it. He'd have noticed that, surely.

In the front of the frame, though, was also a single ticket for the show in Brooklyn Carter had been at. He tilted his head.

"I saw you."

Carter jumped and turned to find Jeremy right behind him. "How do you *do* that?" Bastard had always been too damned quiet.

"Sneak out as often as I did and you develop some mad ninja skills," Jeremy said, chuckling. He plucked the frame from Carter's hands. "I saw you in the crowd and tried to come say hello. You'd gone, though."

"Sorry," Carter apologized. "I didn't know what to say after…"

"After me being a huge dickhead? That's one reason I was so surprised to see you at the show. It, uh, felt like I'd really made it for the first time, seeing you there, knowing you listened to my music at a bar in New York fucking City."

"Sorry I didn't stick around."

Jeremy shrugged, but Carter could tell he was embarrassed by the conversation. Okay, maybe they were getting a little heavy. Carter didn't miss that Jeremy's tan cheeks pinked a little.

He also didn't the fact that Jeremy's bare chest was covered in gooseflesh, his nipples nicely pebbled. His cock gave a small show of excitement, but that was about all it had for now.

"I liked that one song. I have the whole album, but I'm lame like everyone else and only really know the one."

Jeremy feigned a wounded heart. "You didn't listen to my angsty melodies and swoon for me?"

Carter stilled. Was the guy just stoned or did he mean that? "Was I supposed to?"

Again, Jeremy's cheeks had a slight pinking to them, which was wholly unlike him.

"Actually, most of my angsting has been for Troy. But I just had my hand on your dick, so we probably shouldn't talk about this."

Carter didn't disagree. He did want to know more eventually, though why it mattered, he didn't know. For now, he definitely didn't want to talk about Jeremy's old hook ups. He was still smarting a bit from Jeremy spending his morning with one.

"So, what's it to be? More *Downton*? *Upstairs, Downstairs*?"

"Oh, Jem, you sure know how to woo a girl."

"I got everything you need, Red." Jeremy gave carter a wink and squatted down to turn on his gaming console that doubled as his Blu Ray player.

Yes, you do. Carter could get on board with a change of pace. He'd gotten off, Jeremy was all smiley and cute—and deliciously shirtless, showing off his massive amount of ink on his torso, shoulders, and arms. He could go for some couch time.

They settled in on the couch, Jeremy being more affectionate than Carter thought he'd be, but he chalked it up to Jeremy being tired.

Then Jeremy slipped his cold hand in and held Carter's junk, making him jump. "Hey!"

"Warm up my hand, bae."

"Don't call me 'bae', *bae*."

"Hush, the show's starting."

Carter sighed.

And he really tried not to focus on how much he enjoyed this, reminding himself that this wasn't his life and he wouldn't be here for much longer before getting back to reality.

He could enjoy it for now. There was no harm in that,

right?

10

The next couple of days went much the same. Jeremy's dad hadn't hung around much, dealing with clients took up a lot of his time. But Carter enjoyed seeing Jeremy spend more time with his mom and Sarah.

Sarah and Carter had gone into Chattanooga to see old classmates a couple times, but for the most part, days were spent around the farm, working the horses and hanging out with everyone during the day, and Carter and Jeremy just shooting the shit and blowing each other when everyone else was in bed.

Carter thought Sarah and Daphne knew more than they were letting on, but given the smooth sailing lately, no one seemed to want to rock the boat by acknowledging anything.

Jeremy had taken to working out with Carter in the mornings, which was probably most telling. They didn't have any deep conversations about life or anything, but it felt like they were slowly getting to know one another as friends again. Although, Carter caught himself staring at Jeremy more than was necessary. Okay, mooning over him. It was hard not to, though. The man was physically amazing. And since his personality grew more open every day, Carter saw glimpses of the man he really admired.

He'd even heard Jeremy playing guitar a couple times, singing softly. He cursed the gods on those occasions because it was getting damn hard to maintain a "friend" distance when the man did such amazing things to Carter's body while also being someone Carter saw himself wanting to be around...a lot.

It was so much, but then so little. To an outsider, hell, even to Carter, there was nothing extraordinary about the time they spent together outside the bedroom. The times were quiet and platonic in so many ways. They talked of the band in essence and Carter talked about his travels. But no grand revelations were made.

Still, and maybe it was because Carter had always had a thing for Jeremy, he felt like it *could* be more in a different time or place.

Rolling into the end of Carter's first month of being back home, the elder Becks had gone to Nashville for a getaway and Sarah had a date, so Carter and Jeremy intended to make the most of having an entire afternoon without watchful eyes.

Unfortunately, it had been a long week with many early mornings after very late nights. So after feeding, their work out, and a heavy lunch that Daphne made to get rid of all the leftovers, they were mostly sleepy and ended up doing nothing but staring at the TV for several hours until they passed out without so much as a single orgasm between them.

Carter hadn't realized he'd dozed off until he woke to his phone buzzing. Jeremy was passed out with his hand still down Carter's pants, which made him roll his eyes. He disengaged, trying not to wake Jeremy, and made his way to his phone.

The display showed a missed called from Ella and three from his parents.

There was a text from Ella. *Call your mom. It's been days. She won't leave me alone.*

He responded with a: *I'll call her in the morning. Sorry, Ells. Really.*

It's good. Hope you're enjoying your break. And he knew she meant it.

It was close to midnight. His mother would still be awake, but he was still enjoying his glow from being with the Becks and his night with Jeremy. Real life could wait until morning.

Carter sighed and ran his hands through his hair. He wasn't normally this person. He'd never been the petulant teenager. He'd never fought with his parents. He'd made as few waves as possible until he could get out on his own, but by then, his mother was a nationally known politician so he'd doubled down on keeping his head down. He'd gotten good grades, joined the Army where he'd sailed through because of his fondness for structure and just being glad he was doing something for himself—even if it looked good on his mom's resume for him to join the armed services.

He hated feeling like he was doing something wrong, but he supposed a late bit of youthful rebellion was due him, especially after acting like a sixty year old since he was seventeen.

Dropping his phone on his clothes, which he hadn't realized Jeremy had folded neatly in the chair until now, Carter sighed at himself again. He was being ridiculous if this was the great drama of his life. "God," he said, quietly exasperated.

A strong pair of arms wrapped around him from behind and Jeremy's sleep warm skin pressed against his bare back. "Doesn't care about your petty stuff, there's starving kids in Africa," Jeremy intoned, mimicking Daphne's favorite phrase whenever any of them took the Lord's name in vain.

Carter laughed, but let out a moan as Jeremy ground his hard cock into Carter's ass and slid his hand from Carter's chest down inside his sweatpants to cup his hardening cock.

"Me, on the other hand, I wouldn't mind you calling out my name."

"Do those lines get you laid?" Carter teased, breathlessly.

"Seems so." Jeremy bit down on the muscle that ran from Carter's neck to his shoulder gently, but enough to probably leave a small mark. He started stroking Carter's cock. "You make me so hard with your shoulders. And that ass." Jeremy ground against Carter's ass again to make his point.

Carter's head fell back on Jeremy's shoulder. "Feels good."

"Good. Just think about this. That other shit, it can wait 'til morning."

Carter laughed. "'No drama. Keep it simple,'" he teased.

"Hey, that shit works." Jeremy pushed Carter over to his bed and turned him, pushing him back. Carter laughed when Jeremy yanked his sweats off with one pull. "Straight guys can undo a bra with one finger. I can remove pants with one motion."

"Everyone's gotta have a talent."

"Damn straight." Jeremy grabbed Carter's cock and, without preamble, sucked him right in.

"Fuuuuck." The wet and the warmth was enough to get him hard as fuck, but not enough to get him off. The ultimate tease. Jeremy's playing with Carter's balls sent tingles up his spine. He wanted more, wanted to say things. Which is why he bit his fist instead and moaned.

Jeremy pulled off Carter's spit-slick cock and stroked it with efficient, powerful hands. He used them both, his mouth pressed to Carter's balls. Carter laugh-moaned when Jeremy mumbled around his mouthful to pull his legs up. Carter obliged, and Jeremy's tongue dipped lower. He licked and sucked Carter's taint. He slid one hand down and massaged it as he licked, stroking with the other. Carter's back bowed up.

"Goddamn, Jem."

Jeremy's head came up and he grinned. "You call me Jem when you get all crazy."

"Sorry?"

"Fuck that, it's hot that I get you all out of your head."

Jeremy slid his fingers down to massage Carter's hole

and Carter let out a deep moan. Jeremy dipped just the tip of his forefinger in, letting go of Carter's cock. Carter thrust his hips up, missing the friction.

"So no anal?" Jeremy asked.

Carter swallowed thickly. "I… I still don't…" Although a part of him was screaming, *do whatever you want!*

"Hey, that's cool. Seriously." Jeremy titled his head. "Like no penetration? Just cock or toys too?"

Carter stilled, intrigued. "I've done toys. And fingers myself. But like I said… I haven't been sure…"

"You want to fuck me? I don't mind." Jeremy winked. "I'm easy to please."

Carter swallowed his tongue. He felt lame. That he hadn't fucked anyone ever was probably strange for his age, but he wasn't joking about not being sure about getting fucked, so he'd kind of thought it would be a dick move if he wouldn't reciprocate.

"Really, Carter. I want to if you do. No pressure, though."

Carter just nodded. That earned him an impish grin. "It's kinda hot that I'll be your first."

Something in his chest tightened, but it was nice. He didn't want to be that clingy first timer, but this was one of those things that *did* mean something to him. That Jeremy didn't judge him for not doing more sexually than frot and blowing made him want to hug the man. But he also was glad, even if this was just a short-lived thing, that he'd get to do it with Jeremy who wouldn't judge him if he popped off early or if he was awkward. He knew that deep inside, Jeremy wanted this to be good for him. And he wanted it to be good for Jeremy.

"Let me suck you," Carter said.

"Oh, look who's taking control. I like," Jeremy purred, shucking his pants and bounding onto the bed.

He knelt over Carter's face, positioned on all fours. Now this was something Carter had tried. 69ing he could deal with.

He sucked in the head of Jeremy's cock and Jeremy let out a happy sigh before bending his head to take Carter's cock in his mouth. Carter felt Jeremy moving around, and then heard sounds he couldn't discern, so he continued sucking and stroking Jeremy's thick cock.

Jeremy popped off Carter's cock and said, "Here." He pressed something into Carter's hands. "Get me slick in there. Feel where you're gonna put your cock." Jeremy moved down a bit so his cock was on Carter's chest, ass close to Carter's face. Carter swallowed hard.

Jeremy's ass was spread just enough to tease, his round buns making two perfect mounds. Carter couldn't help himself. He leaned up and took a soft nip of each cheek.

"Oh, fuck yeah. That's nice," Jeremy added. He stroked Carter's cock. Carter smiled, realizing Jeremy was having trouble not being in the lead on this. He might be a virgin when it came to fucking, but he knew what topping from the bottom was and he had no doubt that was how this was going to go.

He smacked each of Jeremy's ass cheeks with one hand while he flicked the lube open, then poured some in his hand. He managed to only dribble a little on his neck, so he counted that as a win.

Twenty-three and fumbling like I'm fifteen. Smooth. Although, he was sure there were plenty of fifteen year olds more experienced with *this* than him at this point.

He willed himself to stop focusing so much on that. It wasn't like he was some untouched innocent. He'd been with a few guys. This was just something new.

As he glanced up the perfect arch of Jeremy's back, over the large cross tattoo and up to the broad shoulders, he thought about *who* was giving him this, who he was doing this with.

He took his lubed fingers and, one at a time, slid them in the tight, warm hole Jeremy was offering. He watched his fingers get swallowed up, watched Jeremy's sides rise and fall with his breath. "Damn," Jeremy whispered. "You ready?"

"Fuck yes," Carter said. He felt cold latex as Jeremy sheathed his cock in a condom and stroked him. Jeremy held his hand out and Carter was almost too distracted staring at his fingers fucking inside Jeremy's hole to realize Jeremy was asking for the lube.

Jeremy made quick work of stroking a lot of lube onto Carter's cock before turning around and squatting with both feet on either side of Carter's hips. "Gonna fuck me good, Carter?" Jeremy's voice was deep and heavy with feeling. His eyes were boring into Carter's, and there was something fathomless about his expression. Carter just nodded.

Jeremy took Carter's cock in hand and held it in place as he settled his hole over the head and bared down. Carter gritted his teeth and curled his toes, trying to keep from going off as he slid into Jeremy's tight body.

Carter rubbed his hands on Jeremy's lightly haired thighs, watching, open-mouthed, as his cock disappeared into this man he'd only dreamed of ever being with like this. His teenage wet-dream was coming true right before his eyes.

Finally Jeremy was sitting all the way impaled, head flung back. The veins in his neck were pronounced as he let out a long moan. Then he looked down into Carter's eyes. "Gonna fuck me good? Give me that cock?"

"Fuck yes," Carter said. Jeremy smirked, because yes, that appeared to be the only thing Carter could say.

Jeremy leaned forward and kissed Carter, just a taste, before leaning back up and rising off, then sitting back down.

"Oh, yeah. Put your hips into it, Carter. Fuck me." He put his hands on Carter's chest and Carter thrust up as Jeremy dropped down. It took a few thrusts to get it just right, but eventually they were moving together perfectly.

Carter leaned up on his elbows and stuck his chin up, begging for a kiss. Jeremy was obviously too fucked out to care about playing the cocky bastard right then and let his lips fall to

Carter's. They moved until Carter was almost sitting, Jeremy's lips to his, Jeremy taking over the riding.

Their skin slapped together, their bodies sliding together. Carter was overwhelmed with the feeling of being *inside* Jeremy Beck. He caught a look in Jeremy's eyes that Jeremy shuttered quickly after realizing he'd been caught. He was glad; glad to know Jeremy felt this—whatever *this* was—and it wasn't just him grappling with how fucking right they felt fitted together the way they were.

God, Darling, here you are fucking someone for the first time and you're practically writing sonnets in your head.

He growled, mostly at himself, and rolled them. His cock slid out, but he pushed Jeremy's legs up and open, aimed his cock, and when Jeremy gave an affirmative nod, he pressed down and slid in with one thrust.

"Ohhhhh shit, that's right. Give me that cock," Jeremy demanded. Jeremy reached behind and grabbed Carter's ass, helping pull him down with each inward fuck. There was no more gentle, no more thoughts of sweet joinings in Carter's head. It was animal and loud and he pounded away. His balls bounced between them, his hands gripped Jeremy's waist as he worked his cock into one of his oldest friends, shamelessly.

"Oh fuck. I'm about to cum," Jeremy announced. His eyes were a little wide, like he was surprised. "You sure you haven't done this before?" He yelped. "Oh fuck, right there. There, there, there!" Jeremy grabbed his cock, stroking fast, and then his whole body tensed, head flung back, hole gripping Carter tightly as cum jetted from the head of his cock.

He was laughing through his orgasm, saying stupid shit like, "Woo hoo. Yee-fucking-haw, Red. Fucking dick it down."

Carter would have laughed, only his cock took over and he pounded and pounded, and his balls drew up. He looked down to where his cock was disappearing in Jeremy like his fingers were earlier. And that was it.

"Son of a...FUCK!" Carter's orgasm made him curl in on himself, burying his cock deep, and he rocked himself inside fractionally as he poured his cum into the condom, deep inside Jeremy.

In the throes of it, both of them convulsing, they moved enough to get face to face and clash their lips together, more tongue than lips, as the position only gave so much. The kisses went from desperate to lazy, then Carter had fallen out of Jeremy's hole and their kissing was almost gentle as they embraced.

Carter's heart was pounding, his skin alive. And it wasn't from having just had the most intense orgasm of his life.

They looked at each other for a moment. Then Jeremy sat up and helped Carter take off the condom. "Well, you got that right out the gate, my friend."

Carter winced at the *friend* thing and the airy tone Jeremy used. Even if Jeremy had felt whatever craziness Carter had, he was doing them both the favor of shutting it down. Carter knew he should be grateful, but one more minute of it wouldn't have killed him.

You're going back to New York. In weeks. Stop.

Jeremy came back from the bathroom, a sated smile on his face. "Well. You wore me the fuck out."

"Yeah." Carter blinked, sleepily. "That was a work out."

Jeremy winked. "Who needs the gym? That was way better." There was something shuttered, less open about his mood, though. Not so much that anyone but Carter would notice. But it was there all the same, reminding Carter to enjoy what he got while he was getting it.

And he'd gotten some grade-A shit, so he sure as hell better buck the fuck up and enjoy it. He smacked Jeremy's ass, which was wide open when he bent over as he scrounged on the floor for their pants. Jeremy jumped up and flipped Carter off before tossing him his borrowed sweats. "Fucker."

"You'd know."

"That was so lame," Jeremy chuckled, crawling in bed with him.

Carter was tired enough sleep didn't elude him long. He did wake once in the night to notice Jeremy curled next to him, hand on Carter's chest. He leaned down and kissed the sleeping man's temple and drifted back off.

He'd wanted to escape reality. It had been nice while it lasted.

11

Jeremy narrowed his eyes when he saw the text on his phone's screen. *I need to talk to you.* Fucking Troy.

He didn't know what the man wanted, but something in him felt like it would be disloyal to Carter to talk to the man about their non-relationship weirdness while Carter was around. He looked up at Carter who was pacing in the dining room, his face serious as he spoke in quiet tones, looking like he was arguing. Probably with his mother. Carter caught Jeremy looking his way and faked a smile before walking out into the sun room.

God, but this had started getting complicated. He wanted to protect Carter from his parents' shit. He knew well enough that no one had been in Carter's corner where his parents were concerned, in a long time. These protective feelings of his were far from keeping things simple, though.

But when he had let Carter fuck him two nights earlier, things had changed, even if he was trying not to admit it.

He hadn't been fucked in a long, long time. Macy liked to watch Troy getting fucked, but she was not okay with Troy using his dick on anyone else. It was a strange setup all the way around, so he couldn't really be upset about it. He'd let it go on too long. He owned that.

He thought it would be easier on Carter to try it first that way. And he thought it would be his chance to get that little benefit since he hadn't bottomed in years. He didn't count on it feeling so fucking special. That it had been Carter's first and the first he could remember since his own first time—he'd been coked out even then—it definitely felt next level, like he had said it would.

Jeremy tried to remind himself that he wasn't going to angst. He always knew he felt things more than he liked to let on, so he'd only been half-joking when he'd said this would be a silly love affair they would tell the grandkids about. He hadn't fooled himself into thinking he was in love, by any means. But this was definitely starting to feel like more than two friends fucking around.

He'd never been so content just... being around someone. It could be the residual high of also getting along with his family again for the first time in ages. He and his dad even managed friendly words.

On that thought, he definitely felt more like a tool. Thinking back on his and Carter's long ago conversation about Jeremy feeling trapped on the outside, meanwhile Carter had no one really, Jeremy realized he had always been on the inside of his own family. He had just pushed them away.

He decided it was time to talk to his dad about something he had been considering. Since Carter seemed like he would be a minute, Jeremy made his way to the main barn where his dad's office was housed.

As much as it sucked to admit he was a fuck up, he had come home to find some clarity. Between his family and a certain redhead, he was slowly getting there. Even if he felt like a lost kid at twenty-five.

He knocked on the office door. His dad called out for him to come inside. He stepped into the office, which was actually much more ornate than one would imagine from the outside. It looked like a headmaster's office at a prestigious private school rather than that of a horse breeder. His dad said it was to impress the high-end clientele. Jeremy called bullshit, though. Dale Beck had been high up the food chain in Nashville's music scene, doing contract law for a couple major labels and managers. He was accustomed to his fancy digs and had carried that over to his new business.

Jeremy walked in, and if his dad was surprised to see him, he didn't show it. Dale was a big guy, taller than Jeremy by a foot. But at some point, he'd gotten old. And Jeremy was just starting to notice it.

"Well, howdy, son," Dale said, seeming to not know whether to be Business Man Dale or amiable friend Dale. The latter kind of surprised Jeremy, but he had been seeing more of that lately.

"Hey, pop. I had a question."

Dale frowned, again looking surprised, but straightened up in his chair and put aside his Mont Blanc to show Jeremy he had his full attention.

"That's a first."

Dale looked down and caught Jeremy's meaning. His face scrunched up as he began to protest. "No. Dad, I didn't mean that as an accusation. An observation. Should have stayed in my head."

Dale subsided. "No. I'll give you, I've always appreciated that I knew where I stood with you, son. Even if I didn't like it."

"Sorry."

"Me too." Dale sighed and leaned back in his chair. "More than you know. But I have the feeling that's not what you came to talk about."

"Actually…" Jeremy sighed, shoring up his pride. "You were right."

Dale's bushy black brows rose into his hairline. "Oh?" Jeremy almost laughed, watching the man try to contain that he clearly wanted to jump up and dance around just at hearing those words from his son.

"Don't look so smug."

"I would never." Dale's lip twitched, but he didn't smile. Much.

"I think I'm done with the band." Dale blinked slowly. Jeremy smiled and continued, "I'm not sure what my options will be. But I wanted you to look over my contract with them and our manager. If you don't mind."

"What do you want to do?"

"I'm not a hundred percent on that yet. I may start something else, contract allowing, or I may strike out on my own."

Dale looked over Jeremy's shoulder, yet there was nothing back there but a wall. He still seemed like he was looking at something. "This a recent decision?"

Jeremy thought on his answer. "Probably longer in the making than you think. I guess I don't know if I can't keep growing with them. I've been enjoying the process on my own. Here."

"Do you have the money to—"

"Dad."

"What?" Dale leaned forward, all business now. Jeremy had to admit, for now, he was much more comfortable with that. He knew how to handle Business Man Dale. Dad I don't hate anymore Dale was a work in progress. "You have to think about startup. And if you're going to stay independent. Will you look for new representation?"

"That's getting a little ahead. I may stick with D&W. I'm just weighing my options." He rolled his eyes, and to appease his father, he added, "And yes, I still have a pretty decent portion from my royalties and my investment in the original corner bar. I would want you to look into that, too. To see if they'd prefer buying me out or if it's in the contract. I won't be broke for a while yet."

"There's always your trust," Dale said carefully.

"Which I won't use, and you know it."

That made Dale smile wide. "Same stubborn son-of-a-bitch." Jeremy's only saving grace for the longest time had been that he'd never cashed in a dime of his trust fund, even after it got turned over to him at twenty-one. His dad had fought it getting turned over, worried he'd blow it on coke or hookers, or doing lines of coke off hookers' dicks.

"And proud of it." He straightened up. "Well, I'm gonna get back to the house. Me, Carter, and Sarah are going into town tonight."

"Alright. Get me that contract ASAP. I'll get to looking over it. Send me your manager's number too. I'll see if she's a haggler."

Lucy? Shit. Jeremy doubted that seriously.

"Cool." He headed for the door, but stopped just as he got to it and tossed over his shoulder, "Thanks, dad." He probably hadn't said those words, sincerely, in a decade. He rapped his knuckles on the door frame and headed back toward the house.

***

Carter sighed as he ended the call with his mother. It honestly hadn't been that bad, but she was becoming more insistent on his assistance with what looked to be an upcoming apology tour.

She seemed as surprised as Carter at his lack of willingness to fall in line like he had in the past. It wasn't even really that he disapproved of whatever it is she and his dad did amongst themselves. He was probably as embarrassed as any kid would be in that situation, but he didn't really give a damn what they did.

What he did care about, still, was how they could have been so hard on him about what they perceived as "bedroom issues"—her gay constituents would love that turn of phrase— when they didn't exactly follow tradition themselves. He had supported his mother, even when he had been mortified to be in the public eye. He had been the good son. He still needed time to let go of some of this resentment. He was annoyed with himself for feeling so childish. He was a grown man, for God's sake. He was a veteran. But right now, just for a little longer, he was tired of being an "old soul", tired of smiling and nodding.

He rubbed his hand down his face. He had to laugh inwardly at the fact he had at one time been judgmental of Jeremy not growing the fuck up, meanwhile Carter seemed to be regressing.

The opening of a door and approaching footsteps drew Carter's attention.

"It's not as dramatic as all that, is it?"

"Not really, no. Just my mom."

"How's the Senator this fine afternoon?"

Carter huffed. "Considering *not* tendering her resignation."

Jeremy's brows went up. "Oh. I thought it wasn't up

to her after…" Jeremy made a face, like he didn't know how to finish the thought.

"Technically, they'd have to go through a process to actually fire her. It's all complicated." Carter pocketed his cell phone. "She wants me to cut my 'little vacation from life' short and help."

"And you told her to fuck herself, naturally." Jeremy said it like he knew Carter would do no such thing.

And Carter hadn't. Certainly not in so many words. "She's not really some villain twirling her mustache, waiting to sick her goons on me if I don't come back. She's just frustrated and I'm being stubborn."

"Which is a positive step if I ever heard one," Jeremy said on a laugh. "I don't think I've ever heard you so much as openly complain about your parents. Even when we were teenagers." Jeremy raked his eyes over Carter in a way that made Carter's cock wake up and take interest. "You don't even have so much as one rebellious little tattoo on your body." Jeremy stepped a little closer so only Carter could hear his next words if someone else were listening. "Not one rebellious bone in your body." He stepped closer, still. "But I'm working on that."

Carter's head fell back and a burst of laughter erupted from his chest. "You're an idiot."

"You love it," Jeremy tossed over his shoulder as he turned to walk back toward the kitchen. Carter blinked, then swallowed thickly as the words *one day, maybe* popped through his mind.

Fuck. No. No, no, no.

He shook his head to erase all that like a mental Etch-A-Sketch. He followed Jeremy when he heard the soft tones of Sarah greeting Jeremy. When he rounded the corner, Sarah waved. "You guys ready to head out soon?"

"I don't understand what you need us for," Jeremy whined. Sarah punched his shoulder, harder than just playfully, judging by Jeremy's grimace.

"The whole point is introducing you guys to my new boyfriend. Trial run for the parentals, and all."

Carter snorted and pointed at Jeremy. "You think he'll be easier to meet first than your parents?" Carter tried to convey with his tone that, no, Jeremy would not take it easy on the guy.

"I'm not that bad." Jeremy couldn't even say the words with a straight face. Carter imagined someone meeting him for the first time. The man had a tattoo over his left brow for fuck's sake.

"Nope. Not intimidating at all," Carter replied drily.

"That's why I wanted Carter there too." She turned to him. "Your timing on this trip is perfect. We've been talking about meeting parents for a while."

"Oh? Must be getting serious." Carter almost cracked up at the scowl his words had made appear on Jeremy's face.

"Yeah. You'll remember him. He was a counselor at that day camp we worked at the summer after junior year." Her smile turned positively evil. "Chris Holder. I believe you were quite fond of his ass back then."

Carter and Jeremy both scowled at her for that, and she cackled. "Jerk," Carter mumbled.

"It's okay." Sarah winked. "It *is* a nice ass." She checked her phone when it dinged and Carter felt his cheeks heat when Jeremy looked at him with a quirked brow. "Anyway," Sarah continued when she finished with her phone. "He was excited to see you again, too. I'd told him about your boxing. He's opening a gym downtown and when I told him about the gym you worked out in up in New York, he wanted to pick your brain about the facilities."

"I'm just an amateur, at best. Not like I can tell him much more than stuff about equipment." Sarah made a *please just get on board* face, nudging her head imperceptibly in Jeremy's direction. Carter rolled his eyes slightly but said "I'd love to." He didn't mind. It was kind of cool he would be seeing Chris again. They hadn't been super close, but Chris had spent enough time with him and Sarah that summer to have considered them friendly.

"Excellent." She gestured between Jeremy and Carter. "It won't kill you two to get away from this damn house, anyway." Opening the refrigerator and looking inside, she missed the way Jeremy raked over Carter with his eyes again.

"Plenty of entertainment around here."

She shut the fridge door and said, "Right. Well, you'll survive one night out, hermits." She opened the bottled water she had retrieved and took a drink before turning back to

Carter. "I'll be ready to leave in about an hour. Don't let that one go hide in his cave just yet." She looked back at Jeremy. "And Chris is driving me back tomorrow, so we can just go in your truck. Please don't go smoke and get too baked to drive."

Jeremy made a childish face, intoning *please don't get too baked to drive.* "Yes, Ms. Daisy. Move along. I'll be ready."

Sarah turned to Carter, who just rolled his eyes and shrugged. When she left, Jeremy asked, "Do you really think they're that serious?"

Carter shrugged again. "Guess we'll find out."

Jeremy's scowl was cute. He wanted to kiss those slightly pouting lips, but thought better of it. Damn, he was getting himself in trouble with his mind playing games, trying to make things with Jeremy out to be more than they really were. Yes, he was having a great time with the man, and yes, they had great sex. But that was as far as Jeremy had said it would go. That was as far as it could go.

"Stop whatever you're overthinking over there," Jeremy said. "Looks painful."

Carter jutted his chin out, trying to gather a little dignity after having been busted being a drama queen. "I'm going to go get ready."

Maybe a night out would be good. He would have to keep his distance from Jeremy. Seemed like breathing room might be a good idea.

12

Walking out of the restaurant, Carter tugged on his jacket. Jeremy's face was still settled in a disgruntled line, which amused Carter to no end. Honestly, the dinner had gone pretty well. Jeremy had been surprisingly quiet, thoughtful, rather than ribbing on Chris.

When Jeremy turned to Carter to say he was going to get the truck and then took off down the sidewalk, Sarah's look was almost incredulous. Carter looked back toward Jeremy, whose long legs, encased in dark denim, ate up the sidewalk. Carter would have to thank Jeremy for wearing those jeans later tonight.

"I thought you said this was going to be some sort of challenge," Chris said.

Carter snorted and pulled his attention away from Jeremy's tight ass, knowing his cheeks were probably bright pink from being so obvious. He wondered if part of Jeremy's being so off his game tonight hadn't been because of how double date-like the whole evening had been. Carter knew Sarah had to be suspicious of their "boy's nights" for all the weight she put on the words when she said them, but he didn't think she would purposefully have set them up like that. Not knowing her brother like she did.

Of course, Jeremy had been off all day, really, if Carter thought about it.

"Yeah. What's up with him?" Sarah asked.

Carter blinked at her. "I don't know why I'd know any better than you." Really. Even if they were fucking around, even if they talked a lot more now, Jeremy was surprisingly deeper than Carter—shamefully—would have thought. Sometimes he felt like he knew the guy better than he ever had before, while some moments made him wonder if he knew the man at all.

Chris looked between them for a moment. "Anyway." He held out a hand. "It's been great seeing you again, Carter. Thanks for letting me talk about the gym so much."

Sarah rolled her eyes. "For half a second, I'd thought maybe Jeremy and I should leave you two alone."

"Hey," Carter said, laughing. "*You* were the one who was all 'you guys will have plenty to talk about.'"

Chris wrapped his arm around Sarah's waist and pulled her close. "And we haven't seen each other in—what—six years?"

Sarah opened her mouth to speak, but the horn of Jeremy's truck caught Carter's attention. "Guess my chariot awaits. It was good seeing you, Chris."

"You too, man. You'll have to come visit once I've got the place up and running for good."

After Carter got in the truck and waved at Chris and

Sarah again, Jeremy started down the road. Carter turned to study Jeremy's face. His expression was mild, but he had the crinkle just at the corner of his eye that Carter knew intimately enough now meant he was smiling, even if not much.

Jeremy looked at Carter from the side of his eye. "What, Darling?"

"Oh, how sweet," Carter swooned, batting his eyes dramatically.

Jeremy sighed, disgruntled. "I can't help that your last name is dumb."

Carter punched Jeremy in the shoulder. "Your face is dumb."

Jeremy reached over and popped Carter in the shoulder. "Don't hit the driver, asshole." Jeremy made to hit Carter again, but Carter put his hands up in surrender, laughing.

"Sorry! Truce!"

"Fucker," Jeremy grumbled, but he had on his real smile now. Carter's chest constricted at the easy, happy expression on the man's face. That he had put the smile there made Carter just a little too pleased.

"God, you can't just go punching people. Your fists are like lead."

"Sorry," Carter said, tone saying *not really*.

Carter studied Jeremy for another moment. It had

been harder than he thought, keeping his hands off the man all night. He was dressed in his typical plaids and rolled up jeans, hair slicked back, showing off his shaved side-part. But these were a step above his usual going out clothes, a finer cotton button down, expensive, dark-denim jeans. He had dolled up, and Carter had to remind himself it had been for Sarah, not for him.

Even if Carter had thought more of Jeremy when he picked out his outfit, no one had to know but him.

"Were you okay tonight?" Carter asked.

Jeremy seemed surprised by the question, then shrugged. "Yeah. Why?"

"Oh," Carter settled back in his seat. "No reason. You were just quiet. You gave Chris minimal shit. I'm impressed."

"Well, even I am capable of growing up," Jeremy said drily. Carter glanced back at him, but the rolled eyes told him Jeremy was teasing. They rode in silence for a while through town, then onto the highway that lead home.

Home.

Carter frowned, thinking how much he had grown to think of the place as home again. He didn't dread going back to New York as much as he thought he would, but his chest got tighter at the thought of giving up Jeremy.

Carter rubbed his knee. Rarely did it hurt these days, especially after having learned his limitations. It had started building to a steady ache the last couple hours, though.

"Hey," Jeremy said quietly. "That okay?"

"Oh. Yes. Just sore. It happens. Not often, but hey, that's why I'm home in the first place."

"I'm sorry, I never really thought to ask you much about it. It's not that I didn't notice the surgery scarring. I guess you just function well enough…"

Carter shrugged. "It's not all that dramatic. I wasn't even injured in action, you know?"

Jeremy was quiet for a beat. "That didn't matter. It scared the shit out of all of us. I almost went to see you."

"Oh?"

"I still figured you were pissed about that last summer. And my parents were on the phone with your parents twenty-four-seven."

Carter snorted. "That's the first time I'd ever seen my parents freak out like… parents. Well, my dad was. My mom tends to be dramatic about things, but my dad was definitely freaked out. Over a biking accident." Carter still, honestly, had flashbacks about that stupid dad on the curved mountainside in Italy where the rain made him lose his balance and catch a spoke to his knee. It wasn't all that dramatic, but the news of a senator's son's mountainside injury must have sounded quite dramatic by the time it'd made it on the U.S. morning news.

"You don't talk about your dad much."

Carter lifted a brow, mostly to keep himself from saying *coming from you*. "Not much to talk about. We get along as well as we always did. You know my folks. Typical boarding school parents. I don't doubt they love me, and I, them. They actually do better now, me being an adult, than they did before. But we've never been *close*. Me with either of them."

Jeremy huffed. "Makes me feel kind of shitty for not being closer with mine."

Carter looked at Jeremy, the hint of regret furrowing the man's brow made him want to reach for him, make it better somehow. Carter didn't know what to say, so he went back to rubbing his knee. Until Jeremy reached over and used his firm thumb and forefinger to rub it for him. Carter sighed, the ache easing. "You're good at that."

Jeremy gave a noncommittal grunt, but kept doing what he did.

The rest of the drive was quiet, save for the soft sound of music on the radio. Carter hadn't even realized he had dozed off until the slowing of the truck, turning onto the back roads that lead to the farm, woke him. Or maybe it was that his knee suddenly felt cool. Had Jeremy's hand been there the entire drive? He had taken it back to use both hands on the wheel for the several turns he would have to do in a short distance to get back home.

"I'll drop you off at yours so you can go to bed," Jeremy said softly. Carter wanted to disagree, wanted to go spend more time with Jeremy, but between the long day and his fully belly, he was too done in to do more than sleep. And Jeremy, while not seeming particularly upset, seemed like maybe he needed time to himself, a good night's rest, or most likely both.

"Thank you," he replied, trying to convey his

understanding.

Before opening his door to get out, Carter was stalled by Jeremy's hand on his shoulder. When he turned, Jeremy's lips were on his. Soft and sweet. The kiss took his breath away, he'd never expected another one with such feeling from Jeremy.

Jeremy pulled back with a smile. "It was a good night." Carter tilted his head. "They're happy. To answer your question." Carter thought back to what he had asked earlier. "I didn't give him a hard time because for once, I didn't want to be difficult."

"Jeremy, don't be that hard on yourself. No one would have thought you were being anything other than … you. Not difficult. You *not* teasing almost made us worry." Carter grinned and winked.

Jeremy smiled back, which was nice, and rubbed his brow where his tattoo was.

"One day, I'll ask about all your tattoos."

Jeremy laughed. "And you'll think I'm ridiculous when I tell you how many were just because. Yes, some have meaning, but… it's just an art. It's an expression for me. Images and words that make up certain times in my life, even not-so-sober ones."

Carter doubted it was as simple as that. Nothing with Jeremy was as shallow as he would lead you to believe with his easy manner and confident swagger. No one who wrote lyrics like the man did wasn't made of deeper waters than that.

"Have a good night, Jem," Carter said.

Jeremy gave a bright smile. "You too, gov'nor."

Carter rolled his eyes, hopped down from the truck, and made his way into his guest cabin.

He looked around, surprised at how unkempt the place was. He'd really taken his *fuck adulthood* bit all the way. He was still living out of suitcases and carry-on bags. Dirty clothes were piled up and there were dishes in his sink from the few times he'd eaten there in the last month. He shook his head.

Never in his short life had Carter lived in such chaos. It may seem a small thing to others, but Carter didn't do things like leave the beds unmade, he had been a soldier. Or kiss a man in his truck, there was paparazzi. And he sure didn't have flings.

The first two, he could work on. The third, he wasn't ready to change. There was a time limit enough in regards to Jeremy, mere weeks left before life and duty would call him back. He thought of Jeremy and how the man was honestly making an effort with his family, even if it was in gradual steps. And Carter felt chastened by the fact he had let himself get so angry at his parents—and at himself, if he was honest—that he let himself go, in a proverbial way.

Suddenly not as sleepy as he had been, he began to organize his clothes, putting away the clean ones and dropping the dirty ones into a hamper to take up to the main house tomorrow. He had been acting like a spoiled asshole for long enough.

Maybe getting other things in order would help him figure out truly what his next move would be, then maybe he could figure out where Jeremy fit in the new order of things. Because it would be nice not to let the man go.

He would not get his hopes up. He still thought Jeremy might have hang-ups over Troy. Just the name made Carter want to gnash his teeth. But he had to be stable again for himself, then he could possibly convince Jeremy their friendship might be stable enough—together— to see if something might come from keeping in touch once they had left here.

Because seeing Jeremy so happy, so quiet tonight because he'd been as content as he'd been thoughtful, had Carter certain he was feeling more than mere lust for the man. Always had, if he was being honest.

He looked over at the clock, realizing it wasn't too late. Step one in getting everything back in order required some heavy lifting and some planning.

Squaring his shoulders, Carter retrieved his phone from his pocket and dialed. On the second ring, he got a, "Hello, sweetheart. I was just thinking about you."

He tamped down on a bitter *I'm sure you were*, and instead said, "Hi, mom. I thought we could talk."

She sighed. "All right." There was a shuffling and she mumbled a, "*hold my calls*." "Sorry. I'm still in the office." Of course she was. But more gently than Carter was accustomed, he heard, "I'm all ears."

"I don't want to get into everything over the phone. And I'm not apologizing for leaving for a while—"

"I don't expect—"

"No, let me finish." He paused, waiting to see if she would try to talk over him again. When she didn't, he continued, "Mom, I love you. But I'm really pissed right now. And probably not about what you think."

"You'd be surprised how succinctly Ella let me know *why* you're pissed. And for the record, I don't blame you. Neither does your father. He didn't know I'd told you to… God, I'm a horrible mother."

"But a brilliant politician," Carter said with more levity than he felt.

"I'd say a pretty typical politician, letting my son down, justifying that it's for the *greater good*. And Carter, I know it's not. I did mess up."

"But you want to retain your seat?"

She was silent for a beat. "Unless I'm forced out by legal means, yes. But if you're wondering if I'm saying the other things simply to get your help with that, absolutely not. Even if I don't entirely blame you for thinking it."

"I don't. Honestly. I never thought you were… that person. I think that's why you telling me not to come out was such a surprise."

"It was—"

"A mistake. I know. I'm trying to forgive. I'll be back home in time for summer classes. I think I'm getting a better clue about what I'd like to do with my life. We'll talk more seriously then. It's still hard to be civil."

"But that's my little Carter," she said, regretfully. "You'd never ever been one for histrionics. Or emotional outbursts. You leaving was so out of character. I'm ashamed how we handled it."

Carter was finished with his understanding for the night. He was worn out again, tired to the bone. "I'll let you know for sure when I'll be back in New York. Maybe I'll layover in D.C. first."

After they had hung up, Carter was surprised how much weight he had lifted off his shoulders. Still, inside him, there was a little boy who wanted to scream and kick and yell at his mother for all the times he had been alone or wanted a hug or just wanted it acknowledged he was gay and that was okay. Because she had never really said it.

But he was a grown man. He had made his choices, his parents had made theirs. The rest might be something for a therapist to figure out, but Carter could say, aside from being a bit directionless, that he wasn't unhappy with his life. Not as unhappy as he had thought months ago. He may not have been out publicly, but his nearest and dearest knew and he had made sound decisions about whom he had given intimate parts of himself—and call it antiquated, but he was still glad about that. Even if this thing with Jeremy was just a fling, his most intimate firsts had been with someone he cared about.

His phone buzzed, a picture message from Ella. It was

a picture of her socked feet propped on their coffee table in their apartment in New York, wine glass and a cheese plate beside them. *Fancy Fridays aren't the same without you.*

And for the first time, Carter could admit to himself that he was missing his life. He loved the break, he loved his time home, but he missed his apartment and his things, and he missed the routine of classes and the gym. And pretty images of Jeremy in his bed having wine and cheese with Carter and Ella on Fridays was enough to chase Jeremy into a restful, if a little hopeful, sleep.

13

"Wait, wait, wait," Chris said, snatching Carter's phone from Sarah's hand. Chris's first dinner with the parents had come and gone and, in the week since, he had spent a couple of afternoons hanging out at the ranch.

Carter reached for his phone, but Chris held it back. Carter looked imploringly at Sarah and Jeremy, but they were both too busy laughing to be of any assistance. Carter was glad to see Jeremy smiling again—even if it was at his expense. He may have looked at the man a moment too long, but Jeremy just winked, still smiling, before Carter tried to get his phone back again.

Since the "date night", Jeremy's thoughtfulness had melted away into that same old camaraderie they had shared the previous weeks. But there was something new to it. There was something more relaxed and open, and he had this kind of quiet peacefulness around him that hadn't truly existed until that night out.

Or maybe it was just Carter's wishful thinking, and having gotten some of the chaos in his life straightened out. He'd insisted to his mother that he would stay a few more weeks, and that when he came back, while he wouldn't do any big interviews or anything, he was officially living his life out and proud and Ella was free of her cloistered life as his fake-but-not-confirmed girlfriend. He even thought he had figured out what he wanted to do with his training, where he wanted to focus his schooling.

But right now, he would deal with the pain in the ass at hand. "It's just a thing we do," he said, realizing he was whining, which didn't help.

"You're telling me that *you*, who was all quiet at camp, then who grew up to be a big bad army boy…." Chris was laughing again and missed his chance to block Carter finally taking his phone back and shoving it in his pocket.

"It's just wine, geez." Carter crossed his arms and settled in front of the small bonfire they had started, sipping on his beer.

"Yeah, Red. Just wine. And cheese. And Golden Girls reruns," Jeremy teased.

"*Et tu*, Jem?"

"You call it Fancy Fridays!" Chris snickered. Carter turned his nose up and drank more.

"You guys, stop picking on him." Sarah turned to Carter. "I'm sorry. I shouldn't have teased." She glared down her brother and her boyfriend. "You wouldn't be making fun of him for not conforming to gender stereotypes, would you?"

"Oh, Jesus," Jeremy groaned. "Here comes the women's studies."

Sarah huffed, Chris laughed until she shut him up with

another glare. Then her lips twitched and Carter threw his hands up.

"Oh, come on, Carter. It is a *little* funny. I imagined you in your uniform being all Carter with his social awkwardness and your rules. Then you come back, and grown up Carter is still playful and does things like Fancy Fridays with his bestie."

Carter shrugged. "Well, in my defense, I only made it three years, and I never was too good in the Army. I was kind of… soft." Jeremy snorted and Carter flipped him off. "Plus, I got injured and my parents were so little help and I was kind of closeted, so Ella and I needed a way to just be ourselves. A safe space."

The whole group fell silent, nothing but the sounds of crickets and the fire crackling. The light breeze blew much warmer these days, but still just a springtime night breeze that required sleeved shirts.

Sarah let out a sad, "Oh," and the guys sat sipping their soda and beer, respectively.

Until Sarah caught that Carter had just pulled the same trick on them. "You bastard!" She jumped up, pointing a finger at him, face twisted in mock outrage. "That's not nice."

Carter chuckled, shrugging. "Payback." *And it wasn't all lies.* Though he was grinning, something in Jeremy's eyes said he knew Carter hadn't been kidding. They sat around chatting, the subject safely off Carter for now. He sure as hell would never be okay with being the center of attention, even if he was ten times better with people than he had been as a shy teenager thrust into his mother's spotlight.

Eventually, though, Sarah was chilly and it was time for Chris to head out, so they took their leave. Sarah hugged Carter and her brother, who both waved goodnight to Chris, and watched them take off in Chris's Jeep down the now-beaten path that led to the back pasture.

It was quiet again for a while, the tall grass swaying in the breeze. The fire had died down a bit and, honestly, Carter hadn't been this content in a very long time. Yes, he'd had moments with Ella or when he had gotten to see things in his travels overseas in his last year in the Army. But this was different, here in this place feeling the comfort of old friends and finally having a little hope for his future again.

And with Jeremy, knowing maybe after this they would go back to his cabin or Jeremy's room and lie around making out. He felt like an adult and a horny teenager all at the same time. *Yay twenty-something.* That made him laugh quietly to himself as he sipped the last of his warming beer.

He rose to go grab another, and Jeremy halted him. "I'll grab you one. I gotta get something." Carter watched as Jeremy walked toward his truck and dug in the cooler in the bed before pulling his acoustic guitar from the extended cab. Carter got a little giddy, because he hadn't really seen or heard Jeremy do more than pluck at the guitar since he had arrived.

He passed Carter the beer, and Carter leaned back on the sleeping bag he had brought to sit on, looking up at the stars, not staring at Jeremy like he wanted to do.

Jeremy's phone went off and Carter almost thought

the moment was over, but Jeremy ignored the call with a grunt.

"You can get that if you need."

"I don't need," he said, sounding grumpy. The shuffling of grass and creaking of the canvas floating chair followed, then the strumming of chords began, then stopped. "You don't wanna go in do you? I'm just messing around over here."

Carter did look at Jeremy then. In the dying firelight, his expression was neutral, but deep in his eyes there was a longing, one he obviously didn't want seen, as he dropped his eyes to look at his finger placement on the strings. The vulnerable moment made Carter's breath catch in his throat. He had waited his whole life for someone to look at him even a fraction like that. Did he dare acknowledge it?

He and Jeremy had been back to their playful, fun fooling around. Would acknowledging that maybe something more was going on here burst the bubble?

"No. I don't need to be anywhere." He hoped he didn't sound as breathless as he felt. Jeremy just hummed and started strumming the guitar strings again. The tune was a familiar, old one. One Jeremy had played when they were teens, a song he had written. Only, it didn't sound folksy like the music of Jeremy's band. It was more pop-y. A little more upbeat, which was something Carter had always thought was distinctly absent from Jeremy's music in the past, that shiny playfulness that lived inside Jeremy had never really shone through in his music.

But now it did, and Jeremy started singing about

taking rockets into the stars and how loneliness wasn't his friend anymore. It was surprisingly light in tone. And Jeremy's voice was mellow and soulful, singing of a man who had been asleep too long and how he had gotten it wrong. He was better now, feeling better. Both bleak and bright, the song made Carter's chest ache because this... *this song* was all Jeremy Beck, and it felt like their whole time together. An amalgam of regret and yearning for the best that was yet to come.

Carter watched Jeremy, unblinkingly, as Jeremy quietly sang the song to its end with his eyes closed.

God. What Carter wouldn't give for more time here, to live closer, to beg Jeremy to come to New York.

But the moment was soon over and Jeremy smiled his cocky smile. "I think I still got it."

"Yeah," Carter rasped. Then cleared his throat and said more clearly, "I like that version much better than the old one."

"Thanks. It just kind of came to me. When I get back to Austin, I think I'll record this solo." *Poof*, the bubble was officially burst.

"Oh? You're going solo?"

"Yeah. My dad's been talking to my manager. The band is going to get another guitarist. I think it's time I moved on. I'm excited about my music again. It's nice. I still have some closure to get, some simplifying to do."

Carter was beginning to despise the word *simple*.

Jeremy started strumming again and laughed when he said, "You know the words." And Carter did. They used to get drunk, Jeremy probably high, and sing *"What's Going On."* It was almost their party trick, because no matter how crazy the night got, pull out 4 Non Blondes, and everyone gathered around for some *Hey Yeah, Yeah, Yeah.*

They belted it out at the top of their lungs and were laughing by the end, like the couple of kids they used to be, like the men who were figuring shit out and had gotten some clarity together lately—if not as a unit, then individually. Carter would stop reading into it. It was the magic of this place and nostalgia.

"Better than fuckin' *Kumbaya*, I tell ya," Jeremy said, still playfully strumming the guitar.

Carter sighed and fell on his back again, looking up at the stars with a wide smile on his face. His head was buzzing nicely. Not drunk, just light and relaxed.

He had just noticed Jeremy had stopped strumming when the man's face appeared over his. That confident smirk, the sexy way he bent down to nip Carter's bottom lip.

"I like this beard you've got going on," Jeremy flirted, kissing Carter's chin, up to his cheek.

"Thought a change would be nice," Carter said, but finished on a moan as Jeremy ground their clothed cocks together. "Mmm, that's nice."

Jeremy kissed him full on, with tongue and sucking lips. He tasted like a hint of marijuana, bitter chapstick, and

Cherry Coke. Carter sighed as Jeremy kissed down his neck. "It's so hard to keep my hands off you for so long," Jeremy said, voice deep with desire. *The feeling is mutual.* But Carter couldn't get the words out as Jeremy unbuttoned Carter's jeans and stroked his cock through his thin boxer briefs. "Wanna taste you so bad," Jeremy groaned.

"Please," Carter sighed.

Jeremy kissed down Carter's chest even though his shirt was still on, then bit his nipple hard through the cotton. Carter moaned. Jeremy eventually made it to Carter's cock and sucked him in. He used his hands to stroke Carter's cock and fondle his balls, and his mouth was like heaven, lips stretched over the head.

He bobbed up and down on Carter, stroking with his spit. Carter's toes curled in his boots. "Fuck, Jeremy. Just like that."

Jeremy chuckled and sped up both his stroking and his sucking, trying to pull the orgasm from Carter. He got Carter right to the edge and popped off his cock.

"God, I need," Carter whispered, unbidden.

"What do you want, babe?" Carter couldn't even tease Jeremy for calling him babe. He liked it.

"I want you to fuck me."

Jeremy crawled up Carter's body, still slowly jerking Carter off. "You sure? You can fuck me again." They had done it a couple more times since the first time, but mostly had stuck to oral.

"Yes." Carter meant it. To his toes. He wanted this to happen with Jeremy. He trusted Jeremy with his first time doing *this*. "I want you to be my first. Is that okay?" He wanted his cards out there about this. Jeremy should know what Carter was asking. Jeremy didn't have to love him in the morning, but tonight he had to know this meant *something* to Carter.

Jeremy looked at him, studying him carefully. "Okay," he replied. The gentle word was almost hard to hear. Carter surged up, taking Jeremy's mouth before Jeremy could get uncomfortable or before he could say something cocky. He wanted that reverent *okay* forever, even if it made him a huge sap.

****

Jeremy's mind was spinning. Surprisingly, not from the joint he smoked before they had come out a few hours back. No, his high was pretty much long gone. The artificial one, anyways. This high was all natural. Adrenaline and nerves and some other feeling he couldn't place his finger on. It scared the shit out of him, the way Carter had looked at him when Carter asked him to be his first. Jeremy had never been anyone's first, and couldn't honestly remember his own first.

He truly thought it was corny as hell when guys made big deals about their first times. But something about knowing Carter was trusting him with this, that Carter wanted Jeremy to be this for him. He wanted to think it was just a *needs must* situation or Carter wanting to be with a guy that he knew wouldn't splash it on some blog tomorrow or hurt him tonight.

No way, though. Not with that steady, sure gaze. Carter had been confident, his chin doing that cute thing it did when he was asking for something that made him feel vulnerable. And that Jeremy knew Carter that well should make him not do this. But God forgive him, he wanted this. He wanted to remember a first time with something, with someone, he was proud of.

"I have a condom and lube in my truck."

"Well, go get 'em," Carter said. The *duh* hung in the air and made Jeremy laugh louder than necessary. The levity was nice. Being around Carter and his sister all night, and harboring this weird feeling toward Carter, was making him sickeningly sentimental and the moment was a little too serious for him.

Not that he wanted to take this too lightly. He *did* respect what this meant for Carter, and honestly, for himself. This was... a thing. But sex was supposed to be fun. Hell, it had been *too* fun with Carter. He was fucking addicted to the red headed bastard. He was growing less and less excited about going back to Austin. He was dying to record, but damn if he wanted to go back to his lonely little apartment.

He jumped up. "Get naked. I wanna see that pale ass when I get back." He started stripping his own clothes off. "Damn it's cold." That didn't stop his hard cock from bobbing up and down, rigid and ready to fucking ride. He stumbled over his jeans as he made his way back to Carter with the condoms and lube.

Carter laughed when Jeremy fumbled onto the sleeping bag, kicking his pants off. "Don't break anything," Carter said.

Jeremy glared at Carter playfully and rolled on top of him, pressing tight as he slotted their dicks together. He rolled his hips, making Carter groan. "That's enough of your cheek, firecrotch."

Carter squawked indignantly, but Jeremy swallowed his response as he licked into his mouth. Carter mumbled, "Fuck," against Jeremy's lips as Jeremy emptied lube into his hands and took their cocks in his fist, lining them up back to back, then stroking them slowly.

Carter's eyes were closed, head tossed back. Jeremy couldn't stop himself from licking a circle around Carter's adam's apple.

Moaning, Carter asked, "Why does that feel so good?"

"Because it's me, of course," Jeremy bragged. Carter rolled his eyes and reached up, gripping Jeremy's hair tightly in his fist, and pulled him down for a rough, take-no-prisoners kiss that had Jeremy's body stuttering, almost busting his nut right there.

"Jesus. Fuck, Carter, you are trying to kill me." He moved around until Carter's legs were open wide, and slid his fingers down to Carter's hole. "We've played down here. You know how to relax?" He knew Carter said he'd played with toys, and they had involved fingers a couple times, so he was mostly talking Carter through the prep. Carter's sexy, prominent adam's apple bobbed as he swallowed, then nodded.

Jeremy kissed Carter's sexy, stubbled chin and slid the tip of one finger inside his ass. Carter hissed. Jeremy checked, and the blissed out expression said this was good. Jeremy slid his finger in that hot, warm hole and twisted it. Carter moaned. Pulling out, he added a second finger, pushing slowly to the hilt. "You want me in there? Want my cock deep inside your hole?"

"Fuck yes."

"You're so tight. Your little virgin ass is gonna feel so good around me."

Jeremy's cock gave a jerk, agreeing with his words even as Carter chanted, "*Yes, Yes.* Want it."

He fucked Carter with his fingers for a moment, making sure to get it nice and lubed up inside, and letting Carter get loose.

When he thought neither of them could stand it anymore, he pulled them out slowly. "Roll on your side." Carter did as instructed. Jeremy curled around Carter's back. "This is going to be easiest for you your first time."

"Please," was all Carter got out. He turned his face and Jeremy leaned up to kiss him. It was a closed mouth, sweet kiss that made Jeremy's breathing hitch. He laid back and rolled on the condom, stroking a huge handful of lube over himself. He could hear the gentle sound of skin rubbing as Carter jerked off, facing away from him.

Jeremy took in the sight of Carter's strong back and well-rounded ass in the firelight. He felt Carter's earlier words down to his knees. *I need.*

He rolled to his side and patted Carter's leg. "Hold it

165

up." Carter complied and Jeremy rubbed his cock between Carter's air cooled cheeks, down into the crack until his cockhead was nudging against Carter's hole. "Take a breath," he whispered in Carter's ear. When Carter did, Jeremy pushed in gently, just the head.

Carter's hole clamped, gripping him so tight he grit his teeth. Carter moaned. "Yes, that's it, Carter."

"Fuck, you're so big. And warm."

"Gonna take it all?" Jeremy asked, wrapping an arm around Carter's chest and kissing his shoulder. Carter moaned, his clenching hole loosening a bit, and Jeremy's cock slid slowly on in to the hilt. They both let out shuddering breaths when Jeremy was pressed balls deep into Carter's body.

"Oh. Oh, Jeremy," Carter cooed. And never had Jeremy's name sounded so fucking right on someone's lips. The grip of Carter's hot body was so fucking intense. All of Jeremy's senses were zoomed in right there where they were joined.

"Goddamn, Carter." Jeremy held Carter, back to chest tightly, both of them breathing hard. Carter's ass clenched and released, clenched and released, trying to get used to Jeremy's girth. He could feel Carter's heart beating so hard, thumping even in his back against Jeremy's chest. He kissed Carter's nape, leaving his lips there, mouthing words he didn't understand himself.

The breeze blew and horses whickered in the background. A car passed on a road far away and the fire popped. The only other sound was Jeremy's heart pounding in his ears and Carter's sweet begging for him to move, to fuck him.

Jeremy wanted to remember every second, every feeling.

"I'm gonna move now."

"Please."

So he did. He pulled his hips back, then pushed back into the almost t00-tight home inside Carter's body. Slowly but surely, he built up a rhythm, helping Carter hold up his leg. He leaned back a bit to get a nice view of his cock disappearing inside Carter, then pulling back out. "Oh fuck, we look so good together, babe."

"Feels so fucking good. So glad it's you," Carter said. His voice was fucked out, Jeremy didn't think he meant the words as deeply as they sounded.

He started fucking in earnest, slinging his hips. Their skin was slapping together. Carter's ass got tighter and tighter on him. "You gonna cum for me? Gonna squeeze my cock and make me cum?"

"Yes, fuck yes, Jem."

The little nickname sent another thrill, one that went in every direction inside his body like a ping pong ball bouncing all around.

"Fuck, give it to me," Carter said, pushing his ass back against Jeremy's thrusts. The pounding of Jeremy's hips made Carter's thick cheeks bounce and that made Jeremy's eyes roll into the back of his head, his cock starting to get that tell-tale itching tingle in the crown of his cockhead.

"Oh, fuck, Carter. I'm getting so close."

Carter twisted until Jeremy was doing his best to kiss him, but there was more tongue lapping tongue than kissing. Then Carter was shouting, Jeremy laughing and then moaning as Carter clenched hard and was cumming with Jeremy's name on his lips.

Jeremy buried in deep so Carter's body wouldn't push him out. And Carter was the most beautiful thing he had ever seen right then, his pale skin, his red hair mussed, the way he looked back at Jeremy with his eyes soft and his mouth hanging open, begging for another kiss. Jeremy clung to him, held him close, fucking in long, deep strokes, and Carter's hole milking his cock.

And then he came. So fucking hard, pushed in deep and saying, "Please, oh so good. Please." He didn't know what he was asking for, what he needed, but he held Carter close, buried deep in him as he shot in the condom and Carter held the hand Jeremy clenched into Carter's pec.

They lay there like that for a long, long moment, catching their breath until Jeremy felt Carter shaking from holding still so long, and he rolled to his back, sliding out of Carter. Carter rolled onto his back beside Jeremy, placing a hand on Jeremy's leg. They lay quietly. Jeremy stared up sightlessly, his mind blissfully empty of all thoughts except how warm and happy he felt in that moment.

Carter rolled on his side, propping up to look down at Jeremy, and he looked so damn well fucked and happy, Jeremy let himself give in and pull the man down for a kiss. He couldn't remember the last time he kissed a man he had fucked and lingered in the afterglow. Hell, he may never have.

His brain switched back on as they made out lazily, and that feeling was back. That yearning, aching feeling he had first felt while he was out with Carter and his sister and Chris the other night. He had felt it before with Carter. Even years ago, he had felt a glimmer of it. But no, it made it almost impossible to breathe. If he wasn't so happy, he would think it was a panic attack.

He just remembered how Carter always felt like... Carter. Safety and home and... Carter.

"You doing okay?" Carter asked, lip quirked in a cute smile. *Cute?*

Jeremy shook his thoughts. "Sorry. Look at me being the one thinking too hard."

Carter's brow went up, then he bent down, lips an inch from Jeremy's. "Freak out tomorrow, Jem." He chuckled as Jeremy snorted and, smiling wide, they kissed again.

14

"Fuuuuck," Carter moaned into Jeremy's mouth as Jeremy held his legs open wide, sliding his cock in to the hilt. They had started out just showering, intending on a quick handjob after their workout, but Jeremy had created a monster. Not that he would complain.

Thankfully, there had been condoms in his gym bag. He had barely had time to suit up and put on lube before Carter had lay on the bed, holding his knees open to reveal his pretty pink hole. Jeremy had done very little more than a finger inside to lube him up before pushing in with one slow, steady stroke.

"Fuck me," Carter said, gusting out a breath that smelled like spearmint toothpaste. The toothpaste he had used after he had blown Jeremy less than a couple hours ago in the gym.

It wasn't even noon yet, but for the last few days since the night in the pasture, they had been going at it every time they got in a room alone. Their time was ticking down. Carter was leaving in just *days*.

And Carter had decided to make up for missed time as a bottom. That was all he wanted to do. Every time Jeremy turned around, his cock was balls deep in Carter's sexy ass and fuck knew he was A-motherfucking-okay with that.

Jeremy pistoned his hips, fucking Carter deep and long. "God, so fucking tight, Red." He looked down, watching in awe as his cock sunk inside Carter. Carter dug a hand in Jeremy's pec and stroked himself off with the other. His eyes roamed Jeremy's body, flicking up to his eyes every once in a while.

They hadn't even played around, now their skin was slapping together and they grunted, chasing their orgasms.

"Fuck, you fuck me so good," Carter moaned. Jeremy got caught in Carter's gaze, his stomach flipping. That was happening a lot when they fucked. It was intense, this need for each other. He didn't know what he would do when their little fling was over. He knew his body would be unhappy, especially when he was back to his own two hands.

Carter clenched inside. "Damn, you're learning."

Carter smirked, then rolled his eyes back when Jeremy changed angles.

There was a knock on the door that led down the stairs and into the garage. He paused, balls deep, and put his hand over Carter's mouth to stifle the moan.

The door at the bottom of the stairs creaked open. "Jeremy, honey, you up there?"

Fuck. "Yeah, mom. Uh, don't come up. I just finished my shower."

"Okay, have you seen Carter?"

Jeremy's eyes widened. "Uh, yeah. He's in the shower now."

She didn't say anything for a moment, and Carter's leveled gaze told him he had just fucked up. "Okay," she said evenly. "Could you tell him his friend Ella's car just came in the front gates?"

"Yes, ma'am."

Everything was silent for a moment. "I'll go wait. Since he's in the shower." Her tone wasn't lost on Jeremy. The door creaked closed.

Carter socked Jeremy in the arm, and he pulled his hand off Carter's mouth. "Idiot."

"You have to excuse me," he pressed his hips down so his now not-as-hard dick drove the point home, so to say. "My other brain was engaged. I could have just said he's being my little bottom boy, give us a minute."

Carter glared, but wiggled and clenched his ass. "Get on with it, dumbass. We only have a minute."

"You're serious?"

"The driveway is long as fuck and you bought us a few minutes. May as well finish what you started." He clenched around Jeremy. "Doesn't seem like you need any help. Fuck. Me."

"You're like a teenager." Jeremy shrugged and started

pounding Carter again.

It took no time before they came, shouting into each other's mouths.

As they got dressed quickly, Carter tossed a dirty look Jeremy's way. "I can't believe you didn't lock the door."

"Hey, my mom never comes up. I didn't think anything of it."

"You've sucked at being stealth since day one. I swear Sarah knows something." Carter covered his sexy round ass, regrettably, with a clean pair of jeans and pulled on a blue shirt that looked surprisingly nice with his creamy white complexion.

Jeremy was surprised the thought his sister might know wasn't freaking him out. Oh well. Carter was leaving soon, so what would it matter now?

He tried not to think on how bummed it made him that Carter's last few days would also be taken up by his friend Ella and the big goodbye barbeque Sarah and Jeremy's parents were throwing.

Jeremy was stopped short from his thoughts as Carter turned to him and pressed a quick kiss to his lips before saying, "I better go catch Ella before Daphne and your mom put carbs in her face and she has a minor stroke."

The laugh Jeremy gave was more a croak than anything as he watched Carter bounce down the steps, so carefree. He put a hand to his lips, still feeling the tingle there.

God, shake it off.

He was being a weirdo.

He finished dressing and made his way to the kitchen where everyone was laughing. He found Daphne, Sarah, and his mother making goo goo eyes at the new addition. His mother and Sarah were beauties, and were known for dressing impeccably, but Ella had a very urban chic look. She was model gorgeous, and with her loose blonde hair flowing over her shoulders, her thin body wrapped in skinny black jeans and a tight black turtle neck and black heels, she looked every bit like the woman Carter would date—if he was straight.

She was stunning and looked like a movie star. And Carter and Ella were so familiar, touching each other, making everyone laugh. They finished their sentences in a way that was almost perfect enough to seem rehearsed, but Jeremy knew Carter well enough to know he wasn't that disingenuous. They also had such an ease about them, you just knew they were in sync. Which sucked hard because as an outsider, they really were couple-y.

And that made Jeremy's teeth gnash.

"Oh, Jem!" Carter waved him over. "Come meet Ells."

Ells. Jeremy walked over, stepping a little too close to Carter, looking Ella up and down. "The girlfriend, eh?"

Ella looked uncertainly at Carter.

"I thought he knew Carter was gay?" Jeremy's mother asked quietly. That made Carter's cheeks redden and Sarah guffaw. Jeremy realized he was practically pissing on Carter's leg in front everyone and *what the fuck are you doing?*

He stepped back, leaning against the counter, crossing one ankle over the other. Ella's eyes flicked between Carter and Jeremy, noticing the obvious wet hair and fresh clothes. She seemed to smirk in the faintest way.

"Okay, Ella, let us show you to your room," Jeremy's mother said. Then she paused. "Unless you want the guest room in Carter's cabin."

"Oh, that's fine. A guest room here is cool." She went to lift a bag but Daphne swatted her off. Carter grabbed the larger suitcase and everyone walked off to take *Ells* to her bedroom.

What is wrong *with you?*

He sighed and went to the fridge for a water. When he turned, he realized Sarah was still sitting at the counter. When he froze, she gave a very exaggerated eye roll of exasperation, then stood. "The girlfriend?" she asked.

He shrugged. "Isn't that what the media thinks?"

Sarah snorted. "That was smooth, by the way."

"What?"

She patted his shoulder as she walked by. "Wet hair *and* he was wearing your shirt. Why didn't you just make out with him on the counter?"

Jeremy glared at Sarah. Okay. So she knew.

She looked a little sad. He didn't want to ask, didn't want to know, so he just said, "I'm going to work on some music. Call me for dinner." He should *not* be that tense that soon after an orgasm.

****

Carter barely had a minute to breathe from the time Ella pulled up. He hadn't missed that little display by Jeremy—who up until that moment, had played pretty nice with everyone. He hated it was directed at Ella, but the fact Jeremy seemed almost jealous gave him an extra thrill on top of his orgasm and the stupid adrenaline from almost getting busted.

He really didn't think they were fooling anyone anymore, but the peace being kept seemed to be so important to everyone.

Ella had barely had time to shower, change, and go with Carter to help Daphne carry things to the grill when old friends started arriving. He wished he'd had a moment alone with her, and a moment alone with Jeremy. But it wasn't to be.

Old school friends poured in. He hadn't realized Sarah had invited most everyone they used to hang out with, but who he hadn't taken much time to get to know in his shyer younger years, save for a few.

Ella came down and brought Carter a beer. "Girlfriend reporting for duty."

Carter huffed out a laugh and took the proffered solo cup. They were going all out. They had pulled out the folding tables and chairs. Music played from the garden speakers. Red checked table cloths covered every table, and they were all full of ice chests and platters of wings and chips and dips.

"This is a legit shindig, huh?" she asked.

"Yeah. I didn't realize it was going to be…" He waved his hand toward everyone milling around the Becks' backyard.

"They missed you." She leaned into his shoulder. "I missed you too."

He wrapped an arm around her shoulders and squeezed. They stood for a minute like that. God, he *had* missed her. She had been his one ally for so long. It was nice having her here.

"I can't wait for you to meet Jeremy. You'll love him when he's not being… himself." He snorted.

"Please tell me you've been hitting that, like every day."

His cheeks flamed and he just sipped the beer in his cup.

"You *have*. About damn time." She shoved his shoulder, making him sway.

"Anyway…" He tried to divert the conversation away from his sex life. Thankfully, Sarah and Chris and another old friend of theirs came over to say hello.

Ella regaled everyone with stories of the snow in New York this year and gallery openings she had been to. It was fun watching everyone seem so in awe of her. It wasn't like they weren't all wealthy as well and didn't do cultural things. They were on an equestrian farm for fuck's sake. But he could see where New York City felt a little foreign, especially the magical way Ella made it sound.

Some of the guys who drifted over seemed to make the assumption that she was his girlfriend. He tried to disabuse them, but eventually gave up because it didn't really matter in the end. She wouldn't hook up at the Becks' home, and she was only here for a couple days.

Carter felt a sinking feeling standing there, drinking his beer, realizing the next time she boarded a plane, he would be with her. After almost three months here, he would be leaving. He would be leaving Tennessee again. He would be leaving Jeremy.

That thought made him look around for the man. Jeremy was standing over with his father by the grill. They were laughing, which Carter noticed had a serene smile playing out on Sarah's lips as she held Chris's hand and watched the scene.

Ella leaned in and whispered, "Isn't that your shirt?"

Carter's eyes bugged out a bit, looking down to see that he was wearing Jeremy's. They had accidentally switched. He looked up at Sarah, who sipped her drink looking like one of those *not my business* memes on the internet.

Chris looked and said, "Oh, did we not know you two

were a thing? Sarah, I thought you said they were a thing."

Sarah laughed. "I said they were trying to be stealthy." She cut her eyes Carter's way. "For months. With Jeremy acting all nice to everyone. Nope. *Totally* didn't know."

Carter felt even his ears go hot now. He glanced over at Jeremy, willing him to come over, but he just looked their way and walked off inside.

"Oh good. Now he's gonna be an ass."

"I don't get it," Chris said.

"He's playing pouty baby Jeremy because he has to share Carter," Sarah explained.

Carter balked. "Can we not talk about Carter like Carter isn't right here?"

Ella took Carter's empty cup and handed him hers that she had barely touched. "Drink your juice, Shelby." She looked at Sarah. "He gets so touchy."

"You're all assholes," Carter pouted. But he drank his beer because he didn't know if his pride could take walking over to Jeremy right then. He saw that annoying, shuttered expression on Jeremy's face. Maybe they had spent too much time around each other. Maybe it was good he was leaving soon. Especially if Jeremy was going to start being a dick again. He couldn't handle, after all they had done, for Jeremy to revert to being a jerk to him or to Jeremy pretending like they *hadn't* been anything.

After another hour or so, the party was even livelier.

People Carter didn't even know, but who he assumed were family friends of the Becks, had shown up. People were well and truly drunk, and there was dancing and plenty of laughter. It was an amazing night. Carter tried not to obsess over Jeremy seeming like he was avoiding Carter.

Carter stopped Sarah twice from saying anything to Jeremy. But eventually, he was annoyed enough on his own. And he had been so excited about Jeremy meeting Ella. He had been looking forward to this, and now he was feeling like a fool because he had almost talked himself into saying something, *anything*, to Jeremy to see if this had to be over when he left. Even if they only saw each other on the odd weekend.

God, you must be drunk to be thinking like this. He stared down into his empty cup and looked over to see Ella chatting with Jeremy's mother and Daphne. He shored up his nerves, and had a decent enough mad-on, that when he spotted Jeremy slipping in the sun room doors into the house, he followed. This was ridiculous. *He had his dick in your ass two hours ago, you can talk to him.*

He followed Jeremy in and was glad to see Jeremy was the only one in the kitchen once a couple of stragglers went back outside. Jeremy was texting furiously on his phone, frowning at the screen. When he put it away, he looked up and saw Carter standing there scowling.

At least he had the courtesy to look abashed.

"Jeremy, what the hell?"

"Hey, Red. Having fun?"

180

"Well, it'd be more fun if you weren't being a jerk to my friend."

Jeremy put his hands up. "I think you're drunk, Red." He laughed. *Laughed*.

Carter didn't want to be psycho or clingy, but damn. "Jeremy, I—" But Jeremy wasn't looking at Carter, his gaze was transfixed over Carter's shoulder. Carter turned to see a familiar guy. Well, he thought he was familiar. The guy had a long beard and unkempt clothes. He looked like he had slept in them.

Jeremy put a hand on Carter's shoulder. "Apologize to your friend for me." Carter looked at Jeremy, trying to figure out what he was doing. "I have something to do…"

He walked over to the guy and the guy hugged Jeremy. Carter's stomach felt woozy all of the sudden. He wanted to yell *what the hell*, but… he wasn't sure what he was seeing. The way the guy held on to Jeremy wasn't exactly platonic, either, when they pulled back from their embrace. He wished he could see Jeremy's face, but he was glad he couldn't, because he'd feel ten types of foolish if he saw that same mooning expression on Jeremy.

Jeremy jerked his head and he and his guest walked around the long way, but Carter knew they were going to Jeremy's room.

"That ass," Sarah hissed beside him. He jerked his head to look at her.

"Who is …" But he remembered that face now, only

last time, the guy's beard had been trimmed and his hair fixed.

"Troy. What is he thinking fucking around with him? With you *right here*."

Carter took a deep breath. "Hey, don't worry about it," he said to himself more than her. He shrugged. "Really, we were just fooling around." He almost convinced himself he wasn't fucking hurting inside. He had almost thought they had been more than just a holiday hookup.

No. You were. But he was in love with Troy. Doesn't mean you meant less. "It's just over," he said, shrugging again.

Sarah looked baffled. "Come on," he said. "Let's go back to my party." He was damn well gonna get drunk enough to not think about what Troy and Jeremy were doing on the bed upstairs.

But then… *No.* He remembered all the times Jeremy talked about how Troy had fucked him over, how much Jeremy had been hurt by Troy treating him like a play thing just to help Troy and his girlfriend have a little kink in their lives.

He was going to deal with this. Even if he wasn't going to fight for Jeremy's hand like a silly rom-com hero, he would at least remind him that Carter was his friend and Carter cared. And that Troy was a mistake, even if Jeremy didn't want to be with him.

But he didn't want to walk in on anything. He didn't think he could handle that. Plus, that seemed like a conversation for a more sober time. He would talk to Jeremy tomorrow.

For tonight, he would go pretend his heart hadn't just broken into a million pieces. And who knew he had gotten than far involved?

Yeah right.

15

Jeremy was… put out. His first thought toward the entire evening was how put out he was. He couldn't understand why he had almost shoved that Ella girl down when he saw her getting hugs from Carter. Then when he got Troy's text message saying he was driving in tonight of all nights, he'd been just… annoyed.

He had never been truly annoyed with the man. Troy had seen him through his final days of detoxing, had been with him as they started the band. Had been the only guy he'd had feelings for when he had been sober for the first time in years.

But tonight, he wanted to be back in his room watching stupid shows and laughing with Carter. Alone.

He had felt that old warmth as Troy hugged him, sure. And leading Troy up to his room felt like a promise, an old promise.

But he was so… something.

That damn feeling.

Jeremy had sat twiddling his thumb for ages, waiting for Troy to shower. He had been ripe from driving for hours. His mind kept wandering to the party in his backyard.

Eventually, Troy came out from the shower. He was clean, at least. He didn't look quite as rough as when he had arrived.

He watched Troy look around his room and realized the bed was still unmade from his and Carter's earlier fucking. He hurried to make it, then sat, feeling a little overwhelmed by everything going on tonight.

After taking a moment to try to gather himself, he finally looked at Troy. "So."

Troy looked worn out. He hadn't shaved or slicked his hair. He turned an uncharacteristically shy smile on Jeremy. "Hey."

Jeremy blinked. "Uh. Hey."

"Can I?" he nodded toward the bed Jeremy sat on. Jeremy didn't really know what to say, but like all the times Troy had texted while Jeremy was spending time with Carter, when Troy sat where they had been intimate, he felt a strange stab like he was betraying Carter. *Where we were intimate?* He didn't know where that thought came from. They'd had rough, crazy, almost-busted sex. Yet here he was thinking in terms of intimacy.

God, he remembered the confusion on Carter's face all night as Jeremy brooded in his jealousy. Shit, he had been a jealous bastard and here he was … What must Carter have thought when he saw them come upstairs?

But what did it matter? Carter's friend was here to take him back to New York. Tonight was his going away party. And here was Troy.

"Me and Mace broke up."

Jeremy's head jerked to look up at Troy. "What?"

"About three weeks back. That's…" He grunted. "That's why I've been trying to get in touch with you."

"Oh." Jeremy didn't know what to say. "That sucks."

It was surreal. He had hoped to hear those words for a handful of years. But hearing them was different than he thought it would be. He always figured he would do a jig. He had spent so long pining for this guy, or something of the sort, because Jeremy Beck does not *pine*. But now? He felt sorry for his friend.

"I hate that for you," he said honestly, and put his hand on Troy's knee.

Troy's shoulder slumped, almost in relief. "God I've missed you, Germy."

He grimaced at the nickname. "I've missed you too, man."

Troy leaned into Jeremy. There was an old comfort, a balm from being close to Troy again. He knew this man. He had fucked this man.

But as Troy turned his big, soulful, sad eyes his way, flashes of Jeremy's own hurts, the way he ached after each time he had fucked Troy in front of Macy, then had to watch the couple get off together after he had finished. He always felt dirty. And used.

He stood. He needed to catch his breath as all that hurt flowed over him.

Troy reached for him. "Hey, J. Sit with me."

"I need a minute." Suddenly, Troy's presence was stifling. And he didn't get it. This was something he had thought he wanted.

Troy stood and his beautiful green eyes bored into Jeremy's. "I need to apologize."

Jeremy stood still as Troy placed a hand in the center of Jeremy's chest. "You do?" His breath stuttered. Troy had only touched him like this in the early days, before Macy, before they had gotten complicated.

"I called Milo. And I was bitching about you not answering the phone and… he fucking laid me out. He told me how much I had fucked with you head." Troy gripped both of Jeremy's shoulders, his eyes imploring. "I didn't get it, Germy. I didn't."

"Stop calling me that." He didn't know where that came from.

Troy stepped back, but kept his hands on Jeremy's shoulders. "I'm sorry."

Jeremy closed his eyes and sighed. "No. I'm sorry. I just… I don't understand what you're doing here."

"You want to leave the band."

Jeremy scoffed. "That's what this is about? Really?"

"No! When Lucy told me you were wanting to leave, I realized… I can't do this shit without you, J. I can't. And I realize my weird closet shit has hurt you and… I can't. Not without you."

"So Macy gets the boot because?"

Jeremy wanted to hear it and didn't know why. It was probably cruel. He didn't know what was even happening but… something irrevocable was happening and he needed it.

"Because it's you. It's always been you."

"Are you high?" Jeremy couldn't stop himself from asking.

Troy laughed his old easy laugh, and no, he wasn't high. And then his lips pressed to Jeremy's. And the birds… didn't fly and his heart stopped. But not in the way he ever thought. He felt this deep down shame. *Why are you doing this?* He saw each moment of Carter standing in the field with his red hair shining in the sun, a happy smile on his face. He saw Carter warming him up because Jeremy was shivering and scared. He saw Carter watching him play music in a bar in Brooklyn.

He saw Carter walking away and remembered the sinking feeling as he watched him go, and the desolate, false high of touching Troy later that night.

Troy pulled back and looked at him, confused. And suddenly it was simple. So fucking simple.

Jeremy dropped on his ass on the bed and… he laughed. He laughed from hysteria, and from some humor, and a whole lot of feeling like an idiot because he thought about how stupid this little *ah-ha* moment was.

"Oh, my god," Jeremy said, laughing louder. He felt this weight flying off his shoulders and then he felt stupid because for a guy who preached and lived by his whole *keep it simple* creed, he had been the one to miss how simple everything actually was.

Troy sounded quite offended when he said, "What the fuck, man?"

"Oh, Troy." Jeremy was laughing so hard he had tears leaking from his eyes. "Jesus. I'm an idiot."

"Awesome."

Jeremy stopped himself as best as he could and grabbed Troy into a huge hug. "I'm sorry, Troy. This really isn't about you."

He pushed Troy back. "Honestly. I've just been making shit so complicated."

Troy's brows went up, obviously thinking Jeremy was insane. "Clarification would be nice."

"I'd love to explain it to you, but really, I have something I have to do." He took Troy's cheeks in his hands and planted a huge kiss on his lips, then quickly left, running down the stairs, laughing the whole way.

His first realization that he had been dealing with Troy longer than he had thought was that it was very dark out. Then he saw the crowd was very thin outside, and Daphne was swaying as she danced alone, singing as she put dishes in the dishwasher.

Slipping in behind her, feeling fucking buoyant--yes, he felt like one of those smiley-faced helium balloons-- he kissed her soft cheek. She started, but laughed as he took her hand, spun her around, and danced with her for a minute.

"What's gotten into you?"

"Sense," he said.

She snorted. "Well, that's been a long time coming."

"Hater."

"Brat."

"You win," he said, grinning.

She stopped, a happy grin gracing her face. He realized she hadn't looked at him like that in ages. She was almost more of a mother to him than his own. And in reality, his mother had been a good mom. Daphne had just actually travelled some of the bad days with him, when even his own mom had been finished with him.

She put a hand on his cheek, still studying his face. "You okay, baby boy?"

He took a deep breath and nodded. "Yeah. Sorry. I'm being a bit of a drama queen—"

"You?!" She held a hand to her chest dramatically.

"Shush, you." He looked out the window. "Where's

Carter?"

Her smile dropped. "Oh. Hon, he left."

"What?"

"That's why the party wound down. I figured they told you."

Jeremy stepped back, blinking. "Where were they going?"

"He had to go see his dad." Jeremy turned to find his dad looking at him quizzically.

"His *dad?*"

Daphne said slowly, "Yes."

"Holy. Shit." Carter couldn't leave. Not now. "When did he leave?"

His dad looked at him like he'd gone a little crazy. Maybe he had. He felt like it. "Son, maybe you should slow down and tell us what's up?"

"When did he leave?"

"An hour ago?"

"A fucking hour?!" Jeremy's voice squeaked. Okay, he deserved the wide eyes he was getting from Daphne and his dad now.

He ran up to his room and grabbed his phone and his keys. Troy tried to stop him, but he didn't have fucking time.

He practically tripped running back down into the house, but he'd left his keys on the counter. Both his parents and Daphne were standing there. "What airport?"

"Airport?" his mom asked. "What?"

"Son—"

"Dad, not now." He thumbed through his phone, but other than a *What r u thinking?* from Sarah, there were no messages. "How could he not tell me he was leaving?"

His mom sounded as lost as Jeremy felt. Lost wasn't the word. He was fucking bereft. "Well. It was sudden. And they're just—"

He ran out to his truck and was about to jump in when his dad grabbed him by the back of his shirt. "Son, would you wait just a goddamned minute."

"Dad!"

"Drama queen. This is why everything goes to hell in a handbasket around here," his mother grumbled.

"No. Listen to me, guys," Jeremy practically wailed.

"No. *You* listen, for once in your damn life," his dad said, looking annoyingly amused.

"What the *hell* is going on?" Sarah snapped, walking up on the other side of Jeremy's truck. Ella walked up behind her, looking surprised.

Jeremy's heart stopped. Right there. Bringing up the rear, looking a little bleary eyed and a whole lot of confused, was one gorgeous redhead.

"Your brother is losing his mind for some reason," Jeremy's mom said.

Jeremy rounded the truck and grabbed Carter, trying his best not to shake him. "They said you went to see your dad."

Carter grimaced. Obviously Jeremy had shaken him a little. Oops. "Um. He's at my cabin. He showed up—"

Jeremy was over this. He kissed Carter. In front of God and everyone. He pulled back a little. "I'm sorry." He kissed him again. "So fucking sorry."

****

Carter couldn't tell if he was drunk, or if Jeremy was drunk, or if he was dreaming, or…

"What?" he asked. But Jeremy's lips were on his again. Fuck, though, he couldn't help but melt. Jeremy was kissing him. One of those real, *welcome home* kind of kisses. With their chests pressed together, Carter could feel Jeremy's heart beating so fast, so hard.

Carter's eyes opened and behind them, he focused on the entire Beck family, plus Chris and Troy. A shocked audience. *Embarrassing, party of 2.*

"Jeremy, what are you doing?"

Jeremy stopped. Really stopped when Carter held a hand out to make him take a second. Then Jeremy Beck's cheeks flushed a deep red as he turned back to his family. "Oh. Wow. This... Sorry." But he turned to Carter and gave him a shove. "What the hell, they said you left!"

"The party. We said he left the party," Dale said.

Carter suddenly felt the embarrassment of all the attention on him and seeing Troy, he remembered Jeremy had ignored him all night, the humiliation of Jeremy taking Troy up to his room. Carter looked over and scowled at Troy, who looked as lost as Carter felt. Then he narrowed his eyes and looked at Jeremy.

And punched his arm.

"What the *fuck*, Jem?"

Jeremy rubbed his arm, but he was smiling. "I love you."

Carter blinked so much his vision blurred.

"Um. How about let's..." Dale said, clearing his throat. Everyone seemed to take pity on them and started going inside. Though, Carter noticed Troy looking particularly chagrined. Maybe he felt a *little* satisfaction at that.

When they'd all gone, even though the curtains were twitching, and a few folks straggled in the backyard dancing drunkenly to Patsy Cline songs on the speakers, Carter turned to Jeremy. "Say what now?"

Jeremy, who *never* looked ruffled, who was always the

picture of confidence, was… lost for words. It was a moment Carter was afraid to revel in because not two hours ago he had been preparing himself to leave Jeremy behind and let him get his shit together on his own.

"I love you."

Carter stood still, not realizing he was holding his breath until Jeremy scowled and said, "Dammit, breathe."

Carter exhaled and felt dizzy for a second. Jeremy kissed him again and Carter thought for a second that maybe he was just losing his mind. But the kiss felt so real. "How?" he heard himself ask.

Jeremy looked at him, looking as sad as anyone Carter had ever seen. "I'm sorry you have to even ask." He took Carter's hand and pulled him toward his truck, letting the tailgate down. *Our redneck love affair.*

That made Carter giggle. *Ok. Maybe I'm still a little inebriated.*

The smile on Jeremy's face was so serene, it made Carter really, truly get how serious Jeremy was. "I don't understand."

"Turns out, I'm a bit of a drama queen."

Carter quirked a brow.

"Okay. I'm usually better at doing this with music. Which sounds dumb, but I'm gonna try this."

Jeremy took a deep breath. "Life to me was always *so*

heavy. The angst of being a rich kid. The angst of feeling everything *so* much. I kept thinking if I just simplified my life, stop looking at me like that, I know you're tired of hearing 'simple.'" Carter smirked at Jeremy.

"It was why I thought no one loved me. You tried to tell me. Even as a teenager, you tried to show me that love isn't always dramatic. Sometimes it's messy. But most of the time, it's as simple as blood, or as just being there for each other. But, while I thought I was so laid back and so chill, turns out I'm really just another angsty asshole looking for big declarations and flashing signs.

"If I thought I was in love with Troy, maybe it was because it was … intense or a hot mess or whatever.

"But over the last few weeks, I had this *feeling*, this thing that I couldn't put my finger on because it was me and you and nothing was on fire and nothing was blowing up. There were sparks during sex, but the rest of the time it was just us laughing.

"Then Troy kissed me—" Carter puffed up at that, but Jeremy held a hand up. "Please. Let me get this out. Please?" Carter scowled, but nodded, because wow.

"Sometimes love is just in the quiet moments, it's in support and friendship and wanting to be with someone because they feel like home. Hell, I'll use my favorite word again: simple. Sometimes love is found in the simple things, the simple times. When you find a love that doesn't hurt, that doesn't mean it's not real. Hell, it sneaks up on you that way. It's how I didn't even realize 'til I realized I was about to throw it away for something complicated, and more than that, something ugly."

Jeremy took a breath and Carter sat trying to absorb it all.

Then Jeremy put a hand on Carter's cheek. "So I have a choice. Do I want to run looking for the heavier, the intense, the scary? Or do I want the quiet love looking me right in the face?"

Carter tensed. "So I'm… the lesser of two evils."

Jeremy laughed, but it was a sorrowful, sad laugh. "Never. You're the fucking stars and home and I'm not going to marry you tomorrow, but you're that love I found when I was too young to get it. And I thought love was supposed to hurt, and because you *never* hurt me, it was hard to see you. And that you never have done anything but wanted to just be there, no questions asked, is scary in its own way. I see you, Carter. And if you can even give me a chance, I want to love you and spend more time with you."

Carter felt like an idiot for the way he choked up. But he gave his best watery smile. "I don't like you, Jem." He kissed Jeremy. "I've loved you forever. I may not have always been *in love* with you, and I may not have gotten it myself at times. I feel dumb because you *did* hurt me, but you were sitting on a stage singing your heart out once, and I knew then you were more than just Sarah's spoiled older brother." He chuckled. "And that was the *longest* I love you ever, by the way. And probably the most I've ever heard you say at once."

Jeremy laughed, equally as watery now. "It had to be." He put his forehead to Carter's. "It took me so long to get to you, I had to make it the longest apology I could. You deserve pretty words. I am a musician, after all."

"You're an idiot," Carter said fondly.

And they kissed. Full of home and stars, and it was simple. And it was good.

And then Sarah opened the window and the wolf whistles started.

They pulled apart, laughing. "So Troy's here," Carter said.

"Uh. So your dad is here…."

"Oh, shit!" Carter exclaimed.

15

Jeremy woke the next day and smiled when he saw Carter passed out on the bed beside him. Carter was still fully clothed and his pompadour was no longer gelled, but a fiery red tangle of hair all over the place. Carter's cheeks were puffy and lined from the imprint of the pillow case.

And Jeremy didn't want to run screaming from the room. His heart beat a steady, peaceful rhythm, cheeks aching from smiling at his ridiculous looking Red lying next to him.

He never thought he would have a moment of such clarity as he did the night before, but if that had been telling, this was a revelation. He was happy. *Fucking* happy.

Throwing his arms and legs over Carter—Jeremy *was* naked—he wrapped around the man and clung, shaking him a little. Carter groaned.

"Wake up."

"Fuck off."

Jeremy burrowed his face in Carter's neck, nipping at the warm skin, then licking a line from neck to cheek. Carter whined, sleepily, and tried to push him off. But Jeremy didn't miss the grin trying to break free.

"So mean, Red. That was the fastest honeymoon period ever." Carter just grunted. Jeremy leaned up just enough to look down at where Carter's long, strawberry blond lashes fanned on his cheek. Carter's nose scrunched as he closed his eyes tighter.

"I didn't even get a blowjob after my big speech," Jeremy whined, shaking Carter more, rubbing his hard cock against Carter's clothed hip.

"Because being a pest is going to change that?"

He licked Carter's ear. "It has every other time."

Carter eyes opened just so he could roll them. "Who knew being a pain in the ass was a turn on."

"I'd have used it years ago if I'd known it was so effective. Much easier than writing songs and cheaper than plying people with booze."

"You're such a slut."

Jeremy rolled onto his back and threw his arm over his eyes. "You wound me." He reached down to fondle himself. "I don't know if I can keep it up now."

Carter snorted but continued lying still. Jeremy knew he was being a little ridiculous, but the day before had been stressful, and—Carter's dad showing up—had made for a hell of a tense night.

The Senior Darling had slipped quietly into town to apologize to Carter and announce he and Carter's mother would, in fact, not be pursuing a chance for her to stay in office. *"We caused enough grief, and worst of all, we cause you grief. Maybe it's time we took some time to re-examine why she wants to do the job. And no doubt about the fact, we need to reevaluate our relationship with you."*

Jeremy had stood behind Carter and he had put his palm on the small of Carter's back as Carter stared at his dad, seeming to not know what to make of either his dad's sudden appearance, nor his obviously real regret. When they had left Carter's dad in his cabin and gone back to Jeremy's room, they had ended up being pulled into a few more minutes of hanging out with Sarah, Chris, and Ella--who it turns out was pretty nice-- now that Jeremy was over himself. Well, as over himself as he got.

And Carter had turned to Jeremy, put a hand over Jeremy's where it rested on his knee, and smiled such a genuine, in-love smile before saying, "Thanks for being there with me." Jeremy had felt ten feet tall. Sarah and Ella had covered knowing smiles, but even theirs had pleased him. He knew he would still fuck up, but knowing he had gotten that simple thing right for Carter meant the world to him.

Lying in bed, next to Carter, he wanted to touch him. *Really* touch him. And he wanted a few more minutes in their space, just the two of them, before they were thrust back in with the gossip hounds, otherwise known as their friends and family.

After a moment, Carter's warm hand reached out, rubbing Jeremy's hip. The simplest touch, but it sent such a thrill through Jeremy, he couldn't believe he hadn't realized what it was, long ago. *There's your sign, idiot.* So many signs that had been there before. But like Carter, they were no-frills,

201

tangible things. And it felt like saying Carter wasn't exciting, but that wasn't it. Carter was intense and beautiful and... everything. He was all those things without having to be the most all-consuming thing in the room. Jeremy did enough taking up space on his own, it was crazy to realize Carter was the balance to that.

He rolled until his lips pressed gently to Carter's sleep-warmed mouth. It was a brief, firm pressing together, and Carter's hand slid to Jeremy's aching cock, then he fondled his balls. "God, Carter," Jeremy whispered, looking in Carter's blue eyes. "I just... I love you."

Carter looked at him with that same loving expression as last night, but not a little wonder. "The way you look at me, Jem. You mean it, don't you?" Jeremy nodded and Carter gave an exasperated sigh. "How can I tease you for being annoying when you're... this."

Jeremy smirked. "Less teasing, more of that happy stuff you're doing with your hand. We have to face the music soon enough."

Carter snorted but rolled on top of Jeremy, lips to his, tongue licking into Jeremy's mouth. They worked together to get rid of Carter's shirt and shorts. Thankfully, Carter wasn't wearing underwear, so Jeremy's hands slid the shorts off him and had hands full of firm, meaty ass cheeks. He squeezed them as Carter kissed down his jawbone, moaning when Jeremy slid fingers over his hole.

"Who's the slut, huh?"

"Fuck you," Carter retorted with no heat, other than

the horny kind. Jeremy hissed as Carter pressed their pelvises together and started grinding, cock slipping in the tight space between their stomachs.

"I thought you wanted me to fuck *you*," Jeremy said throatily into Carter's ear, this time sliding a finger down, pressing the tip inside Carter. Carter bucked.

"*Fuuuuck*, that's nice."

"Yeah?" Jeremy nipped Carter's bottom lip, sucked it in, and pressed his finger all the way inside Carter. Carter moaned, ass clenching. "Yeah, you do like that. For someone who wasn't so sure about anal…" He stopped and grimaced. "Sorry, you know I'm not *really* picking on you for waiting, right?"

Carter's mouth had been open, head back. He dropped his forehead to Jeremy's. "It was always just about the right person."

That Jeremy knew Carter meant he was the right person made his heart pound, sent a need, a spark of desire that was startling and something he would have made fun of anyone else for in the past. But fuck it. He pulled his finger out of Carter and wrapped Carter in a tight embrace and lazily made out with him, their cocks tensing between them with each roll of their hips.

Eventually, Carter pulled out of the kiss, eyes wide with desire, and started fumbling and twisting sideways to reach inside the drawer of the bedside table, coming back to kiss Jeremy and pressing a condom in his hands. "Put it on."

"Bossy."

Carter huffed, leaning back, pouring lube in his hands. He put his feet on either side of Jeremy's lap, then lay, legs splayed between Jeremy's, and fingered himself, getting himself slick inside with lube.

His eyes never left Jeremy, who licked his lips and watched those long fingers as Carter fucked himself on them. Jeremy stoked himself, then put on the condom. Carter passed him the lube and they lay there beating off, Carter also fingering himself, looking each other in the eye. It was heady, and Jeremy wanted to look away but couldn't seem to force himself to.

"Come on, babe. Sit on it," Jeremy said, gripping himself, holding his cock straight up.

Carter just nodded, and pushed himself to a squatting position. He held his balls up and stared down as he lowered onto Jeremy's cock. Jeremy was transfixed watching himself disappearing inside Carter's body. And knowing why he felt the way he felt, knowing why his body *needed* Carter, made every nerve sing.

When Carter was fully seated, he leaned forward and Jeremy leaned up on his elbows so they could meet in a kiss. The kiss was graceless and perfect. Jeremy drew up his knees, and together they started rocking. It took a second, but eventually they found a rhythm and switched between a slow grinding, a rolling of the hips, and a pounding that drove the breath right out of Carter, gusting over Jeremy's lips. Their eyes stayed locked and their mouths inches from each other. Carter's hands rested on Jeremy's shoulders as he used them to work himself on Jeremy's cock.

And Jeremy felt so connected in that moment, more so than he ever had with any other human.

Their skin was slapping and sweat dripped between them. Soon Carter was jerking himself and Jeremy dropped back on his pillow, gripping Carter's ass cheeks, pounding up into Carter as Carter slammed down on his lap.

When Carter came, it was on a sigh. A loud sigh, but a contented one, his body clenching around Jeremy. And all Jeremy had to do was watch Carter's face, feel the splatter of Carter's cum, and he was burying himself deep, shooting into the condom, gripping Carter's ass to hold them tightly together.

Carter fell on him, Jeremy's cock slipping out, but that didn't matter as their lips found each other again and Carter whispered, *"I love you,"* as he kissed Jeremy over and over, gripping his biceps tight, like Jeremy might float away from him.

"Hey, hey." Jeremy stilled Carter. "I'm here, okay? I'm not going anywhere."

Carter's sex flushed face seemed to get a little redder before he pressed their cheeks together and they laid there, chest to chest, letting their breathing even out.

Jeremy stroked down Carter's back, every once in a while making a pass over that perfectly toned ass. He started humming to Carter, until he thought maybe Carter had fallen asleep. "Carter?"

Carter pushed up and smiled timidly. "Sorry, it got a little intense."

Jeremy kissed Carter's stubbled chin. "No. It was perfect."

Carter rolled on his side and looked at Jeremy. "What do we do? I'm still a little surprised at everything. I believe you. I *want* you. But… we haven't really talked logistics."

"Well, you go back to New York. You have to finish school."

"Yes. That's pretty non-negotiable. I'm in a good school. And I've only got two semesters left. Especially now that I know what I'm doing. And what I want to do definitely brings me back here, in the end. I want to be here, to be home. But for now, I like my life in New York."

"You'll have to fill me in." Jeremy sat up and pulled off the condom. "Be right back." He needed a moment. If he did a happy dance in the bathroom, no one need know.

He walked back out and passed Carter sweatpants and a shirt, pulling on some of his own. "You know my dad got me out of my contract with the band. I had to sell my stake in the bar, too. So my bank account it sitting pretty right now." Jeremy hated to bring him up, but he had to. "That's why Troy showed up. He was pretty unhappy about me getting out of D&W. But it's time."

"What're you going to do next?" Carter sat cross-legged on the bed, and Jeremy put a hand on one of his thighs.

"I'm going to work on my own music. See if I can

make anything of it. My dad and I... we've had some great talks, and I trust him to help steer me toward the right people."

Carter's brows lifted high. "Wow. I mean, I knew things were getting better. I guess..." Carter lifted Jeremy's hand to his mouth and kissed his knuckles. "That's great. I'm glad things are getting better between you guys."

Jeremy shrugged it off, but he was pleased, and knew his smile probably gave it away. "Seems we're both making headway in the parental department."

Carter looked off as if in the direction of the guest cabin. Jeremy couldn't stop himself. Damn it. He had to kiss that wistful smile. "We're gonna die of diabetic shock."

"Yeah, well. Honeymoon phase and all. I'll be back to giving you shit soon enough."

"I have the feeling you'll be back to it when we're at the table with my sister."

"Probably," Carter sing-songed, rising from the bed and disappearing into the bathroom.

Jeremy checked his phone while he heard the sink running and teeth being brushed.

There were a couple missed calls, more than one from Troy, who'd left during Jeremy's big "I love you" speech to Carter. But there was only one text. From Milo.

Dude! Troy is freaked, but I'm stoked for you! Call when you're done making like bunnies.

He was not looking forward to all those *I told you so*s.

Carter came out of the bathroom and smiled at him.

"Ready to face the firing squad?"

Jeremy groaned, but before he could fall backwards on the bed, Carter had taken both his hands and pulled him to standing and kissed him thoroughly. And Jeremy now knew what it was like to be kissed until you were weak in the knees.

Jeremy looked at Carter, and in all seriousness, had to ask, "Do you think if we'd talked earlier or... I don't know. Were we not communicating?"

Carter seemed taken aback by the question, then looked thoughtful. "I don't know what we could have communicated. I mean, I could have told you I had feelings, but we really did try to keep it casual, at first. And I think you had to know *what* you wanted to communicate. It seemed like you didn't even really get it until yesterday."

"You're right. I mean, I knew you were something special. Don't think I haven't known that for a long time, okay? And I know I'm... me."

"Hey." Carter nudged him. "Don't be sorry. I don't think if one of us had spoken any earlier, the other would have reacted right. Maybe it was just our time. And we have plenty of time, from now on, to smooth over the bumps."

"Damn, you're hot when you're all smart and shit," Jeremy said, kissing the soft spot under Carter's earlobe. Then he grunted, done with the heavy conversation for now. He was still himself, after all. "You think Sarah will be nice to us since

208

we took it easy on Chris that first night?"

Carter guffawed. "Not a chance. And your mom is going to have way too much fun with this."

Jeremy dropped his head to Carter's shoulder and whined, "We could just run away instead."

Carter wrapped his arms around Jeremy's waist and squeezed. "No, but we can tonight. We still haven't broken in the old barn. I'd say that's a fitting farewell."

Jeremy straightened. "Actually, would you mind if I came and hung out for a few days in New York with you? I hear you've got this whole Fancy Friday thing. I like cheese."

Carter looked so damn happy, Jeremy wanted to press rewind just so he could see the blooming of that smile again. He *really* liked getting it right with this guy.

"Of course. Nothing would make me happier."

And wasn't that simple?

EPILOGUE

One Year Later

"I'm proud of your mom," Sarah said, lips quirked in a smart-ass grin. "She only had a small crew of paps at your graduation."

Carter dropped down on the couch beside her, watching as the moving crew carried off boxes. "Yeah, well. It's her version of helping out."

"Most parents write checks. Or give hugs. Yours fires up a publicity machine."

Carter laughed. "Yeah, well. Carrie Darling has her own ideas of what is 'helpful.'"

Jeremy wrapped his arms around Carter's shoulders from behind. "I'll say. Remember when you were going to basic and she had a *write up* in the local paper?"

"Don't remind me. At least this just gets business for the gym."

Carter finished up a degree in business. His parents hadn't been thrilled. It had been too general a major for their tastes, and his express lack of interest in any future dealings in politics caused quite a few tense conversations. But he was going home, to Chattanooga, and he had bought in on Chris's gym. He had been helping expand it with money from his trust. He had also trained a lot more so he could help teach boxing, though he would be more of a figurehead until he got his personal trainer credentials in Tennessee.

"It'll be nice having you back home. Between Jeremy and my husband, I hear more about you moving back than how wonderful I am."

"Oh, heaven forbid," Carter teased.

"Always *Carter this, Red that.* It's exhausting talking about you so much. Even my mom is raring to pick out china patterns for the next wedding."

The choking sounds Jeremy made had Carter laughing loudly, patting Jeremy's back. "Yeah, well, maybe she can let us live together for a while." He nudged toward Jeremy. "And no way am I marrying this starving artist until he's not... um, starving anymore."

Jeremy had left the band, and though it made Carter twitch at first, Milo had come to help him record his first solo album. The sales had been pretty low key, but it had been enough to get Jeremy back out on the road touring. He had come to New York several times to perform at local venues. Carter was thrilled for him because Jeremy seemed like a huge weight had been lifted off his shoulders.

Working with his dad had been good for Jeremy, too. They'd forged a good business relationship, if not totally mended their personal one. They'd definitely done much better than Carter and his parents, who still were all pretty stand-offish because it was hard getting to actually know each other again.

But for all that, Carter found himself even more a part of the Beck family than he'd been before. Even if it had been slightly awkward at first, Jeremy's parents had been extremely supportive of their relationship, especially after Jeremy confessed about why he and Carter had been estranged and how losing Carter's friendship, and what he thought had been him losing Carter's respect, had been his wake up call.

Jeremy's mother had visited Carter, along with Daphne, more than Carter's own mother had.

They had all come just days earlier, Sarah in tow, for Carter's graduation. And now Carter and Ella were moving out. Carter was headed back to Tennessee, Ella to an internship in Paris—arranged by Carter's parents.

"Where *is* Ells?" Carter asked absently.

"Oh, she went to help my mom set up for the graduation party everyone thinks you don't know about." Sarah rolled her eyes, then glared at Jeremy.

"You guys can't tell me secrets that I don't know are secrets and expect me not to tell the guy who's literally got my dick in his hands."

Carter nodded. "And he *knows* I don't like surprises because you *all* know I don't like the attention being on me. You're lucky I'm showing up at all."

Sarah put a dramatic hand to her chest. "You'd deny our mothers this moment?"

Carter quirked a brow. "Funny, I could swear this day was about me."

Jeremy snorted. "Yeah. And so was Sarah's wedding day."

Carter and Sarah both winced, remembering the momzilla that wedding had created.

"Speaking of," Jeremy said, standing and holding out a hand. "We should go to my hotel now that the moving guys have everything under control. We both have to get ready." He gave a very not-so-sly wink.

"God. Sometimes I miss when you guys were trying to be all stealth like," Sarah grumbled.

Carter just laughed and took Jeremy's hand. Sarah gathered her things and Carter wandered off to make sure he had the last of his luggage. Jeremy's booted feet thumped in behind him. Jeremy turned Carter and kissed him. "You good?"

"Yeah. It's just crazy how much has changed since this time last year." He looked around his apartment. "I'll miss New York. And this place."

Jeremy waggled his brows. "Me too. We had some wild times in here."

Carter glanced over Jeremy's shoulders to make sure no one could hear. Jeremy rolled his eyes, so Carter leaned in and licked the shell of his ear. "Wanna go put a rebellious bone in my body?"

Jeremy snorted, then laughed out loud. "Oh, Red. I've taught you well."

Carter took Jeremy's hand and walked out of his apartment for the last time. The ride down the elevator was the fastest he had ever remembered it. And that felt like so many moments with Jeremy. Fast and crazy. Though sometimes, it was slow and frustrating. But as he thought about the condo they'd found, the one with the hardwood floors, the short drive to the gym, and just far enough away from the Becks' farm, he was looking forward to every crazy minute they had coming.

Jeremy's dramatic side had this fun, overwhelming capacity to love so hard and so strong, it was almost incongruous with what Carter had thought of Jeremy for so long. Though, it seemed much more like the boy Carter remembered Jeremy had been before sex, drugs, and indie rock and roll. And now, Carter was so at peace in his skin and had a direction, he couldn't imagine life being any different than it had turned out. He felt so different from the Carter he'd been, the one who had spent quiet holidays alone and hid in his apartment.

And it was all from loving Jeremy. Because no matter what Jeremy said, there was nothing simple about their families or their lives over the last year, nor was it simple loving the crazy bastard. Turns out, nothing was better for the introverted prince than being dragged out of his tower by his red hair by a moody, playful musician.

But it was so worth it.

Jeremy had stepped off the elevator when it made it to

the lobby, and when he turned back, the sun was shining through the front door in such a cheesy, dramatic way that was just so... Jeremy for him to practically pose there in it. He tilted his head. "You ready?"

Carter smiled. "Definitely."

THE END

KADE BOEHME

ABOUT THE AUTHOR

Kade Boehme is a southern boy without the charm, but all the sass. Currently residing in New York City, he lives off of ramen noodles and too much booze.

He is the epitomy of dorkdom, only watching TV when Rachel Maddow or one of his sports teams is on. Most of his free time is spent dancing, arguing politics or with his nose in a book. He is also a hardcore Britney Spears fangirl and has an addiction to glitter.

It was after writing a short story about boys who loved each other for a less than reputable adult website that he found his true calling, and hopefully a bit more class. A member of Romance Writers of America's New York City Chapter and Rainbow Writers of America, Kade works as a full time writer.

He hopes to write about all the romance that he personally finds himself allergic to but that others can fall in love with. He maintains that life is real and the stories should be, as well.

Feel Free to Get in Touch With Kade:

Twitter: https://twitter.com/kaderadenurface
Facebook: http://facebook.com/kade.adam
Blog: http://kaderade.blogspot.com/
E-mail: kadeboehmewrites@gmail.com

MORE BOOKS BY THIS AUTHOR

Novellas

*Wide Awake**

You Can Still See the Stars in Seattle (Wide Awake #2)

*A Little Complicated**

*Gangster Country**

Wood, Screws, & Nails with Piper Vaughn

*Keep Swimming**

*Going Under (Keep Swimming #2)**

*Chasing the Rainbow**

Novels

*Don't Trust the Cut**

*Trouble & the Wallflower**

*Where the World Ends**

Teaching Professor Grayson with Allison Cassatta*

We Found Love with Allison Cassatta*

*Chance of the Heart**

SHORT STORIES

Proud Heart: A Chance & Bradley Pride Short

*available in paperback

Made in the USA
San Bernardino, CA
20 April 2016